Edward Garrett

The occupations of a retired life

A Novel. Vol. 1

Edward Garrett

The occupations of a retired life
A Novel. Vol. 1

ISBN/EAN: 9783337046781

Printed in Europe, USA, Canada, Australia, Japan

Cover: Foto ©Andreas Hilbeck / pixelio.de

More available books at **www.hansebooks.com**

THE OCCUPATIONS

OF

A RETIRED LIFE.

A Novel.

By EDWARD GARRETT.

IN THREE VOLUMES.

VOL. I.

LONDON:

TINSLEY BROTHERS, 18, CATHERINE STREET, STRAND.

1868.

LONDON:
SAVILL, EDWARDS AND CO., PRINTERS, CHANDOS STREET,
COVENT GARDEN.

CONTENTS

OF

THE FIRST VOLUME.

———

THE OCCUPATIONS

OF

A RETIRED LIFE.

INTRODUCTION.

THE LAST NIGHT IN THE CITY.

THERE are few things which it is altogether pleasant to do for "the last time." I daresay many brides feel a little heartache when they give their parents the evening kiss the night before the wedding. I think most clergymen would falter a little over a farewell sermon, though next Sunday they were to preach in an ancient cathedral instead of a little country church. And so my heart is not altogether merry as I draw my chair to mine ancient hearth for "the last time."

It is only a lonely hearth in the second floor of a great house of business. The room is rather low, but quite large enough for me; and it has one advantage which I have always appreciated: its windows overlook a narrow strip of grave-yard belonging to a vanished London church. There is a great elm which touches my panes and makes a ghostly pat-tering when the wind is high. I wish the church were still there. One Sunday, its pastor preached in it for "the last time," only he did not know it; and in the week the red flames came, and withered it up before the eyes of the congregation. I have seen a picture of it, and it was a pretty Gothic church. If it were here to-day it would not have a score of worshippers. I should be one; or sometimes I might re-main at home and listen to the anthem and the preacher's voice through my open windows.

I am an old man—I must be, for I have been in this very house, one way or another, for fifty years. I entered as junior clerk— a *very* junior clerk, just fourteen years old. penniless and fatherless, and without home or friends in the great city. But a home was kept for me on the banks of the river Mallowe,—thanks to the courage and industry of my only sister Ruth. She was some years older than me; and when our father died she took his place, and ruled everything for our poor, crushed, feeble mother, with that quiet tenderness which belongs to strong characters. Ruth settled all about my situation, and then she prepared my little outfit, and at last accompanied me to meet the stage coach. Mother did not come further than our own gate. It was a very hot, bright summer-day, and the green lanes and fair meadows looked more tempting than I had ever seen them before. When we reached the corner of the common the coach had not come, and we stood beside the sign-post and talked. Ruth did not exhort me ; she only told me in what parts of my trunk she had stowed away certain treasures ; and at last, when a white cloud of dust in the distance announced the coming coach, she put her hand on my shoulder, and said—

"Now, Ned, never think you are free to go wrong because you fancy it won't hurt anybody but yourself. IT WILL. It will break up our home at Mallowe as much as if it depended on your support and you failed to send money. I shall not have heart to bustle about in the shop and among strange people unless I have cause to be proud of you, Ned."

And then she bent and kissed me, and stood there, smiling, while I climbed the coach. She did not move as long as we were in sight; and very often during my first nights in London I dreamed of my sister standing alone by the sign-post on the broad common.

Yes, Ruth was a wonderful woman. When my father died, people advised that the shop should be given up and a school opened in its stead. That would be proper woman's work, they said, which the business was not. It would have been all very well had it been only the village library and stationery goods; but it was something beside. In or near our village were two solicitors, with large connexions among the farmers and landed proprietors about, and my father kept in his shop all the requirements of their offices, and, what was more, he undertook their copying. He had taught Ruth to help him, and she had been his only assistant, a fact over which there had been much shaking of heads among the old ladies. Of course she must give that up now, they remarked. Ruth said nothing at first, but when they pressed her very

vigorously, recommending particular houses
as suited for her visionary school, and even
giving hints as to what furniture she should
keep, and what she should sell, then she
opened her mouth and spake.

"We know the worst of old things, but
we can't guess the worst of new ones," she
said. "So long as I can I shall keep what
I have."

And so she did. The labours which she
and her father had shared, she managed to
do alone. God knows (I say it solemnly)
how she did it. We had been orphans for
a year before I left home, and her example
during that time was a great boon to me.
She was a living picture of self-denial,
patience, and cheerful industry, all the more
edifying because she did not see it herself,
but was only a little proud of her success as
a woman of business. I fear our mother
never quite appreciated her. But Ruth will
not let me say so. She always remarks,

"Ah, Ned, there was nothing to appreciate; I am very glad that our mother kept me in mind of my faults." But then why was mother so blind to *mine?*—and I might have had many more, and worse ones, and I know she would have continued as blind. Dear mother! she is gone where she is doubtless grown strong enough to understand the daughter who puzzled her so sorely on earth.

London seemed very dismal to me when I alighted from the old "Highflyer." It set me down at the "Saracen's Head," and as I wandered out of the quaint inn yard, I felt a strange sinking of heart. The great world around was so strong, and stern, and remorseless, and I so weak and lonely! It is not at first that we can realize that the vast tide of humanity is composed of little individual waves, one not much stronger or swifter than another, and all, and each (such comfort in that *each!*) carried along by the

pitiful hand of God, who remembers every
face in the vast throng, whether fair or
faded, and knows every heart, and under-
stands all about each life! But at first we
only feel the terror of our own littleness.
Coming from sweet country villages, where
we recognised every one we met, we shrink
from the unheeding crowd, with their blank,
regardless eyes.

I was duly installed in my humble duties
in the counting-house of this establishment.
I don't think I was very bright; but every
one was kind, and ready enough to give a
helping hand to the poor dazed lad from the
country. To me they seemed very clever,
those handsome, well-dressed, gaily-speaking
young men, my superiors. I did not believe
I should ever be competent to fill places like
theirs. As I have said, they were very
kind; but I knew they laughed at me, and
would not care to converse about such
things as I took interest in. For the first

few days this great house was as lonely to me as the streets. But one fair, cool morning, I was told that "the master" had returned from his summer holiday, and wished to see me—little Ned Garrett, from Mallowe. This was the head of the firm,—the other partners had been wisely chosen from among his best and longest-tried clerks. I had never seen Mr. Lambert; but I knew his history—how he was the son of a far-descended fallen country family; how he put aside the prejudice of his rank and entered business life as humbly as myself; how, by God's blessing on his diligence, he succeeded, until at last he bought back the old family mansion, but still remained in business, because he could not bear to give up the influence which he used for good in London. I felt a little awe as I approached his room—this very chamber. It was Mr. Lambert's then; it has been Ned Garrett's since. To-morrow it will belong to somebody else.

He said very little to me. He was a tall, slender man, with a beautiful old face and long silver hair,—no less a gentleman because he was a merchant. He sat in a great brown leather settle, behind a huge writing-table, and he bade me be seated on a little cane chair opposite. He asked if I had heard from home since my arrival, and how were my mother and sister—" your sister Ruth," he called her, and the sound of the old household name was like a breath of the breezes that blow over the sunny Mallowe. Then he said he had heard good reports of me, and he should always like to hear the same, and stretched forth his hand —a white, warm, wrinkled, aged hand—and shook mine kindly, and I knew I might go.

But after that I never felt alone. I generally saw him once or twice a day, only for a minute and quite in the way of business; but that always sent me back to work comforted and content. The great millionaire

—the man who had declined royal honours
—could not hold conversation with such a
unit as me, as he might have done had he
himself been an old clerk with two hundred
a year, and a wife and children in a six-
roomed house at Clapham. The tide of life
breaks into streams, the boundaries of which
it is not wise nor pleasant often to overflow.
But the very character of the man was a
friend to me. From it I could imagine the
counsel he would give, and that it would be
but an echo of the brave womanly words I
had heard under the sign-post on Mallowe
Common. I put the image of the quiet old
gentleman into my heart beside that of my
dark-eyed accurate sister. They were the
lares of my soul. I did not know all this
when I was fourteen, but I know it now.

Well, I prospered, and rose one step
after another, and when I was twenty-
one I was in receipt of a fair salary
for that age. Early every autumn I

took a run down to Mallowe, but not at
Christmas, because in those times we had no
holiday then but the one day. I never
wanted a better change than to go home.
Early autumn was a slack time in the shop,
so Ruth was free to roam the country with
me, and many pleasant rambles we had,
sometimes together and sometimes with
young people from the village, whom I had
known all my life.   Ah, not even in London
had I forgotten one—little Lucy Weston.
I shall not speak about Lucy's looks; I
don't suppose she was a beauty to any one
but me, and I don't suppose she was clever.
She was only a good little girl—a daisy
among women; and we always love the
daisies most, because we knew them best
when we were young! Her father kept
the Meadow Farm, a dear old-fashioned,
gabled house, overgrown with creepers,
which wreathed round its quaint white-curtained lattices, and made the whole place

like a huge nest. Lucy was the only daughter, but she had five brothers, great curly-haired, grinning, tramping, good-natured lads, who came crushing round me to hear about London, until, not having grown much since I first left Mallowe, I always felt quite overwhelmed and breath-less. Yet Lucy was a very quiet thing in manner, and voice, and look. Just to see her was as soothing as to hear an old psalm tune sung softly by little children.

I have not got a vivid memory, but any minute that I like I can fancy myself in the great parlour at Meadow Farm—a long low wainscoted room, with some curious wood-carving about the ceiling and fire-place, and wide windows along one side, beyond which lay a splendid prospect of lane, and field, and hedgerow, mingling summer charms with autumn wealth. The floor was bare, except for two narrow strips of plain green carpeting, which set off the cleanness of the

boards.   There were heavy old chairs with
cushions of some kind of chintz, and a long
well-polished oak table uncovered, except
when clad in white drapery for meals.   The
room boasted no ornaments beyond a fox's
head and brush, and a few firearms over the
mantelpiece, and three great beau-pots of
flowers, one set in each window.   And what a
noise the farmer and his sons made, as they
came tramping in, with loud honest laughter,
and good old jokes that could stand an airing
almost every day, and among them little
Lucy with the breezes in her hair, and her
cheeks a wee bit redder from the family
kisses.   And last of all, "the mistress,"
with her cambric cap and kerchief, and her
broad sunshiny face, that looked as if it remembered all the good harvests and forgot
every bad one.   And then after them came
tea and cake and fresh fruit, borne in by a
stout serving maiden, full of old-school
deference to her superiors, but always able

to throw back a saucy word to the boys, if
necessary. And then we all gathered round
the long table, Lucy and I, somehow, side
by side, and after a moment's hush, there
burst forth the Westons customary tea-
time grace — Lucy's silver voice rising
among the others like a minstrel's harp
amid the clang of martial music—

" Praise God from whom all blessings flow,
Praise Him, all creatures here below,
Praise Him above, ye heavenly host,
Praise Father, Son, and Holy Ghost."

After such a meal as that, on the last
night of my visit in the year of my coming
of age, Lucy and I wandered out upon the
greeny downs behind the house. I was a
little disposed to envy the easy course of
life in that nest-like home, and I manifested
this tendency by setting forth, somewhat
vauntingly, the advantages of city life.
Perhaps I did it to hide my discontent,
perhaps to argue myself into satisfaction

with my lot. But Lucy went straight to the root of the matter. "There's a 'best side,' to everything, Ned," she said, "and there's much to be gained by living in London; but because we grant that, don't let us cry down country life. I'm rather sorry your favourite Mr. Lambert thinks there is so much more to be done among the houses than under the trees. I wish he would come down here and try."

"But life in the country is so narrow," said I.

She looked at me and smiled. "No one can do more than he can, Ned," she answered; "and the narrowest life is wider than most of our hearts. When people have a great many ways of doing good, they sometimes get so confused that they do nothing."

I knew she was right.

"So you have made up your mind never to return to the fields 'for good,'" she remarked, after a short silence.

"I don't say that," I answered. (We were standing on a slight eminence, facing the sunset.) "I daresay you would refuse to live in the city."

"I don't think I should," she replied, shading her eyes; "it would all depend upon circumstances."

"I shall not be able to afford to live in the country till I am quite old," I said—"perhaps not then."

"Well, everywhere is God's world," she answered, turning towards me; then added playfully, "but when you do come, don't make up your mind there's nothing to do but water flowers and go to sleep. There's plenty of work wherever there are sin and sorrow; and sin and sorrow are everywhere. 'The harvest truly is plenteous but the labourers are few:'" and her voice was solemn then.

Ah, pretty Lucy! at the harvest supper some will meet us whom their Father called into the shelter of his own house before the burden and heat of the day!

"Dear me, but I'm grown quite a cockney," I said, after a long pause. "If I am to live in the country again, I shall want some one to show me how."

"You can easily find some one," she retorted.

"Will you?" I asked.

But at that auspicious moment we heard Farmer Weston's lusty voice shouting our names, and Lucy sprang up with damask cheeks, and ran fleetly to the house. I did not see her alone again all the evening. But next morning as I passed the farm on my way to meet the coach, I saw her toying with her beau-pots in the parlour. So I unfastened the wicket, and crossed the garden, meaning to ask for an answer to my question. But the moment I reached the window, Mrs. Weston advanced from the recesses of the room, and overwhelmed me with good wishes for my journey, and an enormous cake and some ripe pears wherewith to beguile its tedium. So perforce I returned to my city abode with an unsatisfied heart.

After a fortnight (scarcely a fortnight—I think it was only ten days) came the accustomed budget from Ruth. It opened with a bulletin of my mother's failing health, and good news of the business, but the third page went on thus :—

"It has been a sorrowful week at Mallowe. Our dear Lucy Weston was taken suddenly ill on Tuesday afternoon. She was unconscious from that time, so no one was sent for, not even her grandmother, and on Wednesday night she died. I know you will be so sorry."

That was all. My sister passed to other topics.

Of course I went as usual to business, but I felt myself worse than useless. The long rows of figures meant nothing to me, and I was blundering on, with flushed, throbbing face, when Mr. Lambert came in.

"You are not well to-day, Garrett," he said, in his soft, modulated tones.

"Not quite, sir," I replied.

He looked kindly at me for a moment. "Have you heard from home?" he asked. "All well there, I hope?"

"All quite well, thank you, sir," I answered.

He sat down opposite me, and wrote a letter. I could feel his eyes upon me now and then. When he had finished, he spoke again :—

"Leave off work to-day, my boy, and take a drive out of town. You're worrying about something—I shan't ask you what. I don't believe it's your fault, so it will be sure to come right again, Garrett." And once more he shook hands with me—the second time since I had been in his house.

I did as he bade me. And I returned, not comforted, but calmed, and strong enough to bear my sorrow. Comfort came by-and-by, but not completely—not till I had been through a simoom of misery which was destined to teach me that I and my first love had been parted by the best and kindest separation which God can ordain.

Ah, Lucy, and it cannot be many more years before I shall hear you singing again; this time a better Doxology than the one in which I can always hear your voice to this very day. I have never forgotten you! Looking upon my life, people might say I did forget, and not too slowly; but where you are, perhaps you know better.

I sent an ordinary condoling message to the bereaved family, and then I settled into my old life, and in due course the time came round for my accustomed visit to Mallowe. I half thought I would not go, but I forced myself not to flinch. I found everything exactly the same. I thought Ruth gave me one or two searching glances, but that was all. I believe it was only my fancy.

"You will go to Meadow Farm this evening, Ned," she said, after tea; "you always gave them the first visit, and they might feel hurt if you didn't now, poor things."

"I shall certainly go," I answered, looking from the window. "Shall you come too, Ruth?"

"I think not," she said. "I am rather busy, so I will stay at home, and then I shall be ready to take a walk with you to-morrow."

The Meadow Farm looked as nest-like as ever, and the beau-pots were still in the windows. But the flowers missed the dainty fingers which had arranged them so well, and they looked faint and drooping. I entered the open door; the house was very silent, but presently one of the brothers, crossing the back-garden, caught sight of me, and came forward to bid me welcome. He was as yellow-haired and ruddy as ever, but his step seemed quieter—perhaps it had grown hushed while *she* lay in her coffin. He led me to his parents. The father was laughing and chatting as usual, but his voice and laugh were those of an old man. The mother's face was as sunshiny, but not so broad. They were seated in their great orderly kitchen. Mrs. Weston explained "that they felt the parlour chilly of an evening; they liked to be where the fire was." The five brothers came in and sat down in a half-circle. Presently the mother spoke about "her Lucy," and her husband joined in. They both shed a tear or two. The eldest brother shaded his face, as from the firelight; another got up and looked into the garden; a third asked if the horse were put up for the night, and then went to the stable to satisfy himself. It was

very touching. They were evidently trying
to pursue their life as cheerfully as possible.
but they could not make it what it had been.
I stayed to supper. The elder brother stood
up and offered "thanks." There was no
singing. "We could not do it at first,"
said the poor father; "it was nothing but
breaking down, and so we got out of the
habit."

That visit did me good : the sight of their
cheerful resignation braced my own soul,
and I returned to London, stronger and
happier than I had been since my last
country visit.

After that, several years went quietly past.
I advanced in the office, until I was fairly a
well-to-do-man, and though still but a
salaried clerk, not without private dreams of
ultimate partnership. At last, when I was
nearly thirty years old, I found myself constantly a guest in the home of a fellow-clerk
—a young man, who lived with his widowed

mother and a sister. Their small neat house at Hackney was very different to great rambling liberal Meadow Farm, and the occupants were as dissimilar. Yet, I believe competent judges would have considered Maria Willoughby much more handsome and talented than the little daisy of Mallowe. Of course, Maria was a town-lady, quiet, polite, and self-contained—a conservatory exotic; while the other was just a little flower, dropped from God's hand, and untouched by horticulturists. But I grew to love Maria—not with such love as I had borne for *her*, but with grave, reverent affection, which would have placed her " in my home and near my heart," and kept her there safe and honoured even to the end. In due time, I opened my suit; it was courteously received, and I believed myself happy in a sensible, middle-aged kind of way.

Well, I don't want to say much about

what followed. Let this suffice. Here am
I, Ned Garrett, a settled old bachelor, and
there is Maria, the wife of a wealthy City
man, the son of a long line of prosperous
merchants. If she had come to me and
said, " I love this man—I loved him before
I knew you;" or, " I see him for the first
time, but I know that I can love him as I
can never love you," I could have forgiven
her and forgotten my own loss and humilia-
tion. But no! Only her mother wrote to
me, saying Maria had received a proposal
from a gentleman who could offer her a
comfortable establishment and handsome
settlements ; and as I could do neither, she
had advised her daughter to act in a way
most conducive to the well-being of all
parties, and Maria had been prudent enough
to consent. Do you suppose I was satisfied
with this ? Not I. I insisted on seeing
the girl, and making sure there were no
underhand dealings or false representations.

But she only confirmed Mrs. Willoughby's letter; and I don't know what I said, nor how I looked, but both women quailed before me, and I have never spoken to either since.

I think that would have cost me my faith in womanhood had Maria been my first love. It was then I learned to thank God for Lucy's grave—for the gentle Hand that had not shattered my idol, but only removed it to a place of eternal safety. And from that time my heart has never yearned for a new allegiance. The bitterness slowly wore away, together with the remembrance of her who caused it. I know that Maria was pretty, graceful, and refined; but her face never comes to me in sleeping or waking dreams—while as for Lucy's, I could draw her portrait directly, if my fingers had as good a memory as my heart!

Not long after that I got my partnership. It was but a sober triumph for me. I wrote

a letter to my mother and sister, and then I
walked out in the darkness alone. There was
no one else to tell. I knew Maria Willoughby would hear the news from her
brother, and I blushed at the coarse pleasure
I felt at her possible mortification, for I was
now in the way to become a much richer
man than her intended spouse. Oh, if she
had only stood the ordeal! Yet even then I
did not wish my success had come earlier
and spared her the trial. One would rather
go without jewels than pass through life
decked out with pinchbeck, in the fond
belief that the glass and gilt were diamonds
and gold. We may regret the baseness,
but not the detection. Let all false things
go!

Not very long after that my dear gentle
mother died. She had been so long ailing
that she slipped out of life almost uncon-
sciously; and I am glad to remember that
her last word was Ruth's name. After the

funeral I remained at home many days, assisting my sister in her final arrangements. Had everything been realized, there would have been a slender competency for her, and I wished her to share my London home, and rest herself for the first time in her life. But she resolutely refused. She would live in the old house and carry on the business, aided now by the orphan daughter of our village doctor. "When I'm an old woman and you're an old man, Ned," she said, "then we will live together if we choose, but not before. You might wish me away if I came. Now, don't exclaim. I should be glad if something happened that would make you wish me away. Shall you never marry, Ned?"

I laughed, and told her, as she was the elder, I was waiting her example.

"Don't talk nonsense," she said, giving an energetic snip to some stuff she was cutting out. And there the matter ended.

But now, after many years, the time is come when Ruth is content to rest assured I shall never need a fresher face than hers for my *vis-à-vis*. For I find the long rows of figures dazzle me, and the new-fashioned ways of business confound my old-fashioned mind. And I also long for green fields, such as that where I talked to Lucy more than forty years ago; and to fortify this failing and yearning, I have argued with myself that it is almost a sin for an out-of-date old fellow like me to keep on grinding and moiling for more gold, which I shall never need for wife or bairns, thus filling a post which might be better occupied by some clever young man with both. So we two mean to live and die together in a quiet country corner; and this very day I have said good-bye to all my clerks, and left some remembrance in the hand of each, just as Mr. Lambert did, thirty years ago, when he came among us for the last time only the week before he died; and I patted the head of a curly-haired lad from Glasgow, the very image of Ned Garrett fifty years ago, and I have told him if he ever want a friend not to forget his old master, buried in a certain snug cottage, where I know even now Ruth is passing about the rooms to see that all is in apple-pie order for my arrival to-morrow.

Yes, I, the old merchant, mean to rest for the remainder of my days. Yet, at the same time, I remember *her* charge, that in the quietest life "there's more to do than water flowers and go to sleep." Ruth will help out my slow comprehension with her keen eyes and clear voice. I only wish there had been a touch of romance about her. It would have made her as perfect as mortals can be. But romance is always sorrow. Therefore, I thank God for my sister's escape.

Now for one more starlit gaze from my

narrow window! To night I see the dim moonbeams over the graveyard of the vanished church, and so far as silence goes, I might be on Snowdon, instead of in the heart of London city; but I know that almost within a stone's throw of my window nestle courts and closes where infamy need never hide its head, even in such polluted daylight as can enter there. I know, too, that in some of the giant houses round me toil men whom the world respects and honours, but whom God ranks with those of other felons who snatch watches to buy bread they are too cowardly to earn. And I own that Lucy's words are true; this vineyard has been too large for me. My heart has not been strong enough for its burden. I have done a little, or rather I have helped others to do it, but it is such a little that I have no temptation to stand where the Pharisee stood, and boast of my good deeds.

To-morrow night I expect to look out on

a far different scene—on quiet meadows
with great hills rising behind them. Perhaps
I shall hear the nightingale below my windows, and the lights will all be out in the
few cottages within ken, just as if each were
an abode of domestic peace and love. But I
must not forget my Lucy's words—" There's
plenty of work where there are sin and sorrow, and sin and sorrow are everywhere."

Yes; God has brought me thus far on my
way, and I can trust Him to guide me to
the end. He never gave me one sorrow
or one pang more than I needed. I find
now that the days which were hardest
to live through are not darkest to remember. I only wish I had known this
at the time, for I was often haunted by a
dreary picture of lonely old age brooding
over memory of sorrow as painful to endure
as sorrow itself. It was my own fault. I
should have trusted God's promises. It

is rather late to begin to have faith, when one is on the brink of the cold river, and can almost see the gleaming gates beyond. But God is very reluctant to say, " Too late."

CHAPTER I.

THE FIRST DAY IN THE HOUSE ON THE HILL.

I LEFT London at dawn, and arrived here before noon. My new home is not at Mallowe, but a little higher up the country, within an easy drive of that dear old place. This afternoon I have taken a fresh survey of my premises, and I am as well satisfied as on the day I bought them, for I am not one to like a thing less after it has become my own.

The house stands on a hill, gradually rising from the river side. Between the trees, by the use of a field glass, I can catch a glimpse of the Mallowe, like a silver thread wandering on a greeny robe. Valleys are very beautiful, with their wealth

of vegetation, and their well-like coolness;
but I prefer the hill-tops. I think a valley
is like youth, a lovely place to saunter for
a while, but where we do not wish to stay,
and where we could not stay even if we
would. I don't say we never wish ourselves back again, for many hill-sides are
very bare and dreary. But age is like a
bower near the summit, whence we can see
the path by which we came, and from
which many things, which seemed ugly
when we passed them, look beautiful in
the distance. And from that resting-place
we can survey the little bit of journey
which still lies before us, and we see that
it is very easy and very short. I know
age is generally called "the descent of the
hill." What! go down to rest amidst the
dampness, and chills, and mists, that always
haunt valleys? No, no.

A narrow scarcely-used road, running between hedges, passes our front door. It

leads direct from our nearest village, or rather attempt at a village, for I saw scarcely a dozen houses as I drove through it. But there are a few great farms standing back from this road, and enlivening it with their sweet sights and sounds. One in particular seemed to come as near as possible to my typical homestead. The dwelling-house stood in a bend of the road, and a long, fair, dazzling flower-garden stretched before the white-curtained windows of the best rooms. At the back lay the farm buildings, loading the air with scents of hay and new milk, and stretching about, as such buildings do, in pleasant places where ground-rents are unknown. A great curly dog stood at the stable door and looked at me reflectively, as if he knew I was a new neighbour whose acquaintance he must soon make. All around stretched broad meadows rejoicing under the warmth of God's hand. I could not resist alighting from my chaise,

and leaning over the hedge. Suddenly I
heard a horse's step in the path behind it,
and a middle-aged man rode up mounted
on a stout cob. He wore light garments
and a brown straw hat, and he looked full
at me as he passed. I almost think he
muttered. I am afraid he grudged my enjoyment of his possessions, for as he left
the field, he shut the gate with a sharp
bang, and rode on to the house. The sight
of his face spoiled my pleasure. He reminded of an old spelling-book picture of
"the dog in the manger." I began to pity
the women who lived in that beautiful
house, with no glimpse of the outer world
except what he brought home to them. I
looked compassionately at an old labourer
who was carting some soil, an ancient man,
with that patient pathetic look which comes
upon the aged when at work. I feared he
never got a single penny more than what
he could legally claim for his poor failing

toil. But, anyhow, he at least knew of
another Master, for as I passed I heard
him singing in a queer cracked voice—

> " The Lord's my shepherd, I'll not want.
>   He makes me down to lie
>   In pastures green : he leadeth me
>   The quiet waters by."

There he paused to raise another shovel-
full, and then went on to the last verse,
as if it and the first dwelt specially in his
mind—

> " Goodness and mercy all my life
>   Shall surely follow me :
>   And in God's house for evermore
>   My dwelling-place shall be."

I was struck by the Scotch version and
accent in an English lane. A few yards
off, a young man was mending a gate, and
from the likeness I concluded he was son, or
more likely grandson to the cheerful patriarch. But he was not singing either psalm
or ballad. His face was quite gloomy—a
handsome face, with noble features, such as

one rarely sees except in the highest or
lowest ranks. He could not be more than
nineteen. Ah, you see I am right. The
old man was near the hill-top, and in the
brightness, but the lad was under the
shadows of the valley.

Another twist in the road brought me to
my own gate. So that surly farmer is our
nearest neighbour? Well, I hope I got a
wrong impression of him. Perhaps, before
this day week, I shall be sorry for my
judgment! I hope so! I hope so!

Ruth was waiting at the wicket, and I
wish a painter had been with me to im-
mortalise the scene—the little red-brick
house standing against the warm greens of
very early autumn, the bright geraniums in
the foreground, the solid pillars of the
entrance, relieved by their snowy stone
globes, and my sister in her black satin
gown, with a lace cap on her head, and a
cambric kerchief fastened about her throat

by the one heir-loom of our family, a little
diamond brooch, presented to our great-
grandmother by the famous Duke of Marl-
borough when he was *fêted* in some town
where her husband chanced to be mayor.
Two prim serving-maidens stood in the
background waiting to do me honour, and I
could hear the deep bay of a house-dog in
the rear. Their decorous faces broke into
smiles when I entered, as if something in
my countenance promised to relax the
reins of domestic discipline. Oh, Edward
Garrett, why are you not dignified? You
and your sister have both been business-
people till now ; you have made a fortune,
and she but an independency, yet she looks
quite a *grande dame*, and you ! do you look
like a gentleman of fortune? Go and see
yourself in the glass, and be humble : your
house, and your sister, and all that is yours,
are too fine for you, old fellow. Go and
hide your diminished head !

Then we had our dinner, and we ate it in
the sunshine, at the open window. Perhaps
it was this, and Ruth's company, which
made it so much nicer than my chop or
steak yonder in the city. We were attended
by a neat-handed Phillis. That is not a
quotation. The girl is really a Phillis—
Phillis Watts, a ploughman's daughter, who
has doubtless derived her fanciful cognomen
from some relative on whom it had been
bestowed by a sentimental fine-lady god-
mother. The other servant came in to help
her to remove the dishes, and not thinking
it right that I, her future master, should
sit by in perfect silence, I inquired her name,
and was answered in a quiet, refined voice—

"Alice M'Callum, sir."

The tone made me observe her more
closely. She is a slight girl, with brown
waving hair, pushed very clearly off her
brow. Her face looked pale and worn
beside the ruddy Phillis. There was nothing

striking in the features, but much in their expression, more particularly when seen in a country-servant. Presently she removed the cloth and withdrew.

"That is a Scottish lass," said Ruth, "and a very superior girl."

"Has she a brother and a grandfather?" I asked, "for I saw two Scotchmen on my road here."

"She has some male relatives who work at the farm below," answered Ruth, taking up her knitting.

"Have you learned much about our new sphere, Ruth?" I ventured to inquire, after a little pause, for she had already resided here nearly a month.

"Really, I have not troubled myself about any sphere outside these rooms, Edward," she replied; "they have kept my hands full until now."

"You have certainly arranged them admirably," I said, looking round. It was no compliment. I never saw better appointed chambers.

By-and-bye I brought out this, my note-book, and began to write. Ruth's knitting needles clicked awfully fast. I know she thought me trifling.

" Is that your correspondence, Edward ?" she inquired, in that cool voice of hers, which always makes me feel so deferential.

" No ; I'm only writing about—about—"

" Your sphere, eh ! Edward ?" and the voice was cooler still.

" Well, yes," I answered, growing despe-rate, " and yours too, Ruth."

" You needn't trouble yourself about mine," she said. " ' Whatsoever thy hand findeth to do, do it with thy might.' That's all the sphere I care about, Ned."

" That is just what I wish to illustrate," I explained.

" The words are plain enough as they stand," said she.

"Yet, Ruth, many seem to read them,
Whatsoever thy hand findeth *not* to do,
fancy thyself doing it with all thy might."

"They are fools," she answered, decidedly

"So are all of us," I remarked, "in one
way or another;" and then followed a long
silence.

"Nevertheless, Ned," my sister began, in
her softer manner, "I own, even the wisest
take long in learning that there is no better
work for them than the bit God puts into
their hands. I know I have often neglected
some duties, because it was out of my power
to perform others."

I could hardly restrain a smile to hear
her use her own shortcomings as proof of
the weakness of "the wisest." But I knew
it meant no harm. It was only a habit
she had acquired through being the sole
responsible person in the old home at
Mallowe.

"And, Ruth," I answered, "there are also people who perform the far-off duties before those near at hand."

"Ah, yes," said she, "like the young woman who could play the piano, but had not learned the use of a thimble."

"And there are still others," I went on, "who yearn after blessings they cannot get, and undervalue those they have."

"Ah, feelings are different to deeds," she said. "To them we can scarcely say 'I will,' or 'I will not.'"

"I think God will help us through our yearnings for what he withholds," I re-marked; "but he will surely punish our undervaluing what he gives, perhaps by making us realise that old school-book line—

'How blessings brighten as they take their flight.'

And speaking of school-books, reminds me that many people will not learn what they may, because they cannot learn what they

would, not knowing that the path of possibility often guides safely through the
maze of improbability; and they seldom
find out their error till too late."

"Yes, truly," assented Ruth, clenching
my meanderings with a proverb :—

> " He who will not when he may,
> When he will, he shall have nay."

And then she rose and went off about some
household arrangement, leaving me to puzzle
out a few more thoughts on the wisdom of
doing first the thing which lieth nearest.

But it would not do. The silent beauty
of the prospect stretching far before my
windows wooed me from my papers, and after
a few ineffectual attempts at perseverance, I
put them aside, got my hat (oh joy! not a
dingy beaver, but a cool, light straw), and
sauntered out. Now, it's just like me to
want to know more about what I know
already. So, instead of turning to the left
and taking the road I had never seen, I

turned to the right and pursued the path along which I had travelled at noon. It was cooler now. The sun was getting low, and the shadows were broader and darker. Very soon I came in sight of the great farm with its outlying houses. The young work-man was still lingering by the gate, which was now mended, and beside him stood a slight figure in white cap and apron. As I drew near I recognised the pale face of my servant, Alice M'Callum. She turned and acknowledged my presence.

"A fine afternoon, Alice," I said. "Do you know, when I saw you at dinner, I fancied I had met relations of yours in the morning, and I suppose I am right."

"This is my brother, Ewen, sir," she answered.

"And you have a grandfather too?" I went on. "I heard him singing the Scotch psalms as I passed."

"Ah, he's always cheerful, sir," she

said, and I thought her lips quivered a little.

" Has he gone to his tea ?" I inquired, looking round, for he was not in sight.

" No," said the young man. " He's just inside yonder tool-house."

The words were civil enough, though rather abrupt, but the voice startled me. Like his sister's, it was a refined voice, yet there was in it a harsh tone of defiance, as if he were ready to direct me anywhere, so as it took me away from him. I looked at the girl. Her eyes were fixed on her brother's face, with an expression of mingled pity and terror. There was something in her countenance which made my heart ache.

" I will go and speak to your grandfather, Alice," I said.

As I drew near the tool-house, the old man came out. Seeing me approach him, and recognising the traveller of the morning, he gave me a sort of half-military salutation, and stood still.

"I find your grand-daughter Alice is one of my household," I said. "She does not seem a very strong girl; but our service will not be hard."

"Alice is quite content, sir," answered the old man, cheerfully.

"Were your grandchildren born in England?" I inquired.

"The boy was; Alice wasn't," replied the patriarch. "Alice was born in the Highlands of Scotland. She says she can just remember the place; but I doubt, sir, that's more from my talk than from her memory. Ah, I see it as if I'd only left it yesterday—aweel!—I don't say it was bonnier than this, nor so bonnie maybe," and he looked round, "but for a' that, sir, to auld folk there's nae place like the auld place."

"What made you leave it?" I asked.

"Ye may well believe, no o' my ain will," said he, "but the Earl, to whose forefathers mine had paid honest rent for a hundred years, took it into his head to make a great sheep farm. So we had notice to quit. Not us only, sir. More than thirty homes were broken up on the same day. One or two hearts were broken, too, I'm feared. Yet the Earl was a kind man, sir, and had never been hard after a bad season. I suppose he didn't know people could care for old walls that had no 'scutcheons on them. I don't doubt he did it never thinking. But that didn't save our sorrow."

"Was there any resistance?"

"No, sir; there were a few fierce words at first, but we understood well enoo' that the Earl could do as he willed wi' his own. And if his agents were kind-hearted folk, why should we make their work painfu' tae them? And if they were cruel, why should we resist what we couldna withstand, and gie them the pleasure o' conquerin', as they were sure to do? We don't like being conquered, sir; if we can't keep a field we leave it."

"And what became of the evicted people?" I asked.

"They mostly went to Canada. All those I've heard of have prospered. If the Earl ever frets about the few old people who were sent to their graves a little before their time, he may comfort himself with the thocht it was a good change for the many in the long run. That's the way the Lord brings good out of evil, sir."

"Your family didn't go abroad?" I queried.

"No, sir," he said. "I had only one son, and his wife was a poor ailing creature, who would have died on shipboard. Yet she had a wonderfu' spirit: there was no one said harder things of the Earl than she did. At the same time, sir, if she could have shown him a kindness, I'm sure she'd hae done it. So, instead of going abroad, we came down here, and my son got a place as manager on a farm, and we all did very well, only the wife died when little Ewen was born. My son lived till his children were 'most grown up. We have had hard lines, sir, since then, but I'm glad he died when he did?"

" Why, how is that?" I inquired.

" Ah, sir, it's a terrible story, and might be better untold. But you seem kind, sir, and however you may judge about the boy, what I can tell will help you to understand Alice."

" Your grand-daughter certainly looks unhappy, Mr. M'Callum," said I.

" She's just witherin' up," said the old man, with the strange pathos of solemn calmness.

During our conversation we had strolled down the lane past the farmhouse, and as M'Callum spoke thus, he paused beside a rude fencing which enclosed a low-lying woody meadow, through which ran a narrow stream.

"It happened there !" he said.

But Alice came running behind us, quite white and breathless. "Grandfather," she cried, "Ewen is waiting for you to go to tea. You know he must make haste back to finish his work," and as she spoke she gave an appealing look, as if she only wished she knew what was told and what remained unsaid.

"I'll come—I'm comin'," answered the old man, with a humility like that of a child detected in some indiscretion. "Mind, sir," he whispered, "it has nothing to do with *her*, except it's hurrying her away to be an angel in heaven."

We retraced our steps very slowly, for the old man was unmistakably feeble. Alice walked by his side in silence. We found Ewen waiting for us where we had left him.

Their home lay down a narrow lane leading from the road. I caught a glimpse of it—a rude wooden cottage, with bulging windows.

"I have put your tea ready, grandfather," said Alice.

"Thank you, my girl; and I'm sure, sir, we're kindly obliged to Mistress Garrett for giving her leave to run out whiles, and do us a turn at housekeeping. Good evening, sir."

"Good evening, Mr. M'Callum," I answered. "Good evening," I added, turning to the young man, but he walked away as if he had not heard.

Alice stepped before me and opened the garden gate. She held it while I passed in. Then she said timidly, "Don't think hardly of my brother, sir. His manner is strange, but he has been through seas of trouble."

"Is he quite ashore now, Alice?" I inquired.

She did not answer for a minute, but her lip and brow quivered. " I'm afraid, sir, it's as right as it ever will be," she said, and burst into tears.

" My dear girl," I began, " I don't want to hear anything you do not wish to tell, but——"

" You'll hear it all soon enough, sir," she said, with a desperate effort to stop her tears ; " but I wanted you to know us a little before you heard."

" Yet, would it not be best for you to tell me your own story ? Why should I be left to hear what other people say ?"

" Then I've got no story to tell, sir," she answered with sudden calmness. " The story is what the people say, and they say a lie !"

There was a clear emphasis in her voice which made me look down at her. Her tears were dried, and her eyes were bright and fixed, like those of a person fronting a railing mob.

"Then I should not heed them, Alice."

"Yes, sir, you would," she replied. Her flat contradiction was quite respectful. She saw life from a position in which I had never stood. She was the wisest in this matter.

By this time we had reached the hall. I held out my hand to her, as Mr. Lambert had given me his on the day I heard of Lucy's death.

"Well, at least, Alice," I said, "remember, I am ready to hear whenever you wish to tell. Do not be too sure that a friend's aid is useless."

She let her hand stay in mine for about a minute. It was very cold. Then she raised her eyes and opened her mouth, so that I saw rather than heard her thanks.

I went into the parlour. My papers still lay about the table, and Ruth had not returned. I wondered if she knew anything of the tragedy of which I had caught a glimpse. I resolved not to ask her about it yet, for I believed she had a practical person's strong dislike to mystery. And what was this mystery? It seemed connected with that handsome, abrupt young workman, scarcely more than a youth. His sister denied its truth, whatever it might be, but I knew that loving women have a happy gift of disbelieving what they choose. Her grandfather had certainly spoken less decidedly; and I could not forget his words as we stood beside that low, deserted meadow, with its sluggish stream. " It happened there." What happened ?

It pained me greatly to see the suffering written on my servant's face. When she brought in our tea she was as composed as possible; but I had been behind the scenes, and I knew there was a reason for her worn cheeks, and for the strange note that sounded occasionally in her voice. Yet what could I do to help her? It occurred to me, I might find an opportunity of speaking to

the young man alone. I know some people
suffer from a strange reserve, which makes
them more willing to open their hearts to
strangers than to their dearest friends. This
arises from a morbid sensitiveness which
cannot bear constantly to meet eyes that
understand all about us. Now this dispo-
sition ought not to be punished or preached
at. It is a spiritual disease, and must be
pitied and cured. At the same time, I
doubt if it ever wholly disappears. To this
day, I am glad Ruth never guessed about
Lucy Weston.

After tea, my sister resumed her knitting,
and as I fumbled with my papers, I caught
her dark eyes watching me with an arch
expression. Presently she said—

"How did you like your afternoon walk,
Edward? Had you any adventures?"

"Hem—no—" I answered, guiltily; "at
least, I met Alice in the lane, talking to her
brother and grandfather. The old man

seems a shrewd, pleasant Scotchman, and he sent his thanks to you for permitting Alice to look after his household arrangements."

" Ah, poor man ! I should think myself a hard woman if I denied him any comfort in my power to give," said Ruth.

"Any special reason for saying so ?" I inquired.

" I believe the young man is as bad as he can be," returned my sister. " There's one very dark story whispered about him in the neighbourhood. He was tried for a fearful deed and acquitted. So, of course, human eyes must henceforth regard him as innocent. I'll not repeat the story, for I don't know any particulars."

" I gathered something of this from their talk in the afternoon," I said. " At any rate, his sister believes him guiltless."

" She's one of those women who are made to be heart-broken," remarked Ruth: "she'd not love him less if she knew him guilty."

"Thank God for such love," I said. "It helps us to understand His own."

"Yes, that's all very fine," returned my sister, "but it seems hard one should be a martyr that others may learn a lesson."

"Yet it is often God's will," said I.

"Well, Edward," she answered, "I don't suppose He wishes it, but as He permits it, of course we must be satisfied. He will make it up to the sufferers in His own good time."

"He makes it up now," I said. "Love is ever its own reward. It purifies the heart which holds it."

"So does fire purify silver," retorted Ruth, "but I doubt if the silver likes the process while it is going on."

"Yet I am sure Alice would not give up her sisterly love even if she could," I pleaded.

"Ah, she can't give it up, so that settles the question," returned Ruth. "There is no laying down the crosses that grow out of our own hearts, and they are always heaviest!"

"The heaviest cross makes the brightest crown," I said.

"I suppose so," she answered. "But when one is over tired with carrying a burden on a long journey, one has not always strength to look forward to the very end. The little bit of road under each footstep is often quite enough!"

"Just so," I said, "and so doing, we shall suddenly find ourselves on the threshold of Home!"

Then followed a long silence. At last I asked, "From what service did you take Alice M'Callum?"

"From Mallowe Hall," answered Ruth. "I knew her by her coming to my old shop, and I always had a liking for her. She was lady's-maid there, and she left because all the servants took sides against her brother, and that she could not bear. Besides she wished to be nearer her relations in their 'trouble,' as she called it. So I offered to take her, and she was quite thankful to come, though our service is much inferior to what she left at the Hall. I told her plainly she was a simpleton. But she only answered 'Never mind.'"

"Well, Ruth," I said, "I am truly thankful you acted as you did. Few women would have courage to engage a servant who expressly wished to be near a relation with 'a very dark story.'"

"I am not in the habit of judging individuals by their connexions," she answered, "and I liked the girl's faithfulness. Besides, for the matter of fear, I may as well tell you I keep pistols."

"Bless me, Ruth!" I ejaculated.

"Well," said she, coolly, turning her needles, and beginning another row. "Better do that, than not do what you wish because you're frightened."

"When did you begin that custom?" I inquired.

"Twenty years ago," she answered; "at the time when I hired a youth to be messenger and odd man about the house and garden at Mallowe."

"Then you took two or three means of protection at the same time," I said.

"I didn't know whether the lad would be a protection," she replied, drily. "He had been a convict, and he hung about the village, saying he could not do anything, because no one would give him a chance. I resolved he should not have that excuse any longer. So I rode to Hopleigh and bought two pistols, and took some lessons in their use. Then I hired him, and he slept in the room over mine. He never knew about the firearms. He thought I trusted him entirely. I think it was a harmless deception. Had he shown himself unworthy of trust he would have found out his mistake."

"Then you were not disappointed in him?"

"No," she said, "he is now highly respectable, and is head man on one of the best farms near the village."

"Ruth," said I, gazing earnestly at her, as she sat opposite me, as upright as a dart, "you never told me this before."

"Why should I?" she replied, returning my gaze with a sharp glance from her keen hazel eyes. "You would have urged me not to do it, or not to do such things again, as the case might be. And yet I'll engage you've been doing the like in London. We're all willing to be a little brave or kind ourselves, but we're prone to wish our friends to shut themselves into safe, selfish cupboards, just to save our own feelings and fears."

"Well, Ruth," I said (thinking this was a good opportunity), "I've come to the conclusion I'll have a little conversation with young Ewen M'Callum myself."

"Very well," she replied, "only you need not speak to him beside pools in lonely fields."

"But supposing the best opportunity occurs in such a locality?" I said, smiling.

"I cannot get into you to direct your conscience," she answered. "But don't follow my example in everything *except* the pistols!"

At that moment Phillis brought in our supper, and our conversation fell into very ordinary channels, until we finally said good night, and retired to our respective chambers.

I wonder if Ruth has really had no romance in her life. I am not so sure of it as I was last night. She is certainly like some apples I have seen, which have green, tart rinds, yet are very sweet at the core. But if God has ever sent my sister one of those special sorrows with which "a stranger in-

termeddleth not," she must have suffered
very much, as such strong natures do. They
always shut their sorrows in their own
hearts, which is very like covering a crown
of thorns with an iron helmet. God bless
her! I almost wish she had been born to
rank and wealth—she seems just the woman
to save a country, like Joan of Arc, or Eliza-
beth, or Maria Theresa.

Yet, after all, but few are needed to do
these out-of-the-way tasks which startle the
world, and one may be most useful just
doing common-place duties and leaving the
issue with God. And when it is all over,
and our feet will run no more, and our hands
are helpless, and we have scarcely strength
to murmur a last prayer, then we shall see
that instead of needing a larger field, we
have left untilled many corners of our single
acre, and that none of it is fit for our Master's
eye, were it not for the softening shadow of
the Cross.

CHAPTER II.

THE MYSTERY OF THE LOW MEADOW.

THE two following days were very rainy, and I spent them indoors arranging my books and papers according to my own fashion. But on Saturday the weather was glorious.

I did not go out until afternoon, and then I made my way down the lane wherein stood the M'Callums' wooden cottage. I found it empty. I could see the glimmer of a fire on the hearth, and a fine grey cat was seated on the window-sill, but the other inmates were evidently out. So I sauntered on.

I had not gone very far before I came to a gate. It led into a field where two cows and a donkey were feeding. It was a clear open meadow, lying full on the slope of the hill, and commanding a fine view of the valley and of my dear old Mallowe. I went in, and rambled about. I attempted a friendship with the cattle, fully believing myself quite alone in the open eye of heaven, when suddenly I caught sight of a man seated on a fallen tree, resting elbows on knees and hiding his face in his hands. It was Ewen M'Callum.

I stood still. I feel an awe in the presence of speechless suffering, for, with all its agony, I know it very often sits close outside the golden gates of God's Paradise. In this case I could scarcely hope so. Yet anyhow there is royalty about anguish. I stood still: and it seemed as if a solemn silence dropped over the meadows.

He sat as if he would never stir, and I scarcely wished him to look up and find me watching him. So I went towards him with a brisk step, and when he raised his head I bade him a cheerful "good afternoon."

He responded and got up, gathering together a little cane and two books which lay near him on the grass. He intended to go away, and I was forced to devise an excuse to detain him.

"This is a fine prospect," I said. " Where does this field lead ?"

" Into the road that goes to Mallowe," he answered.

" I suppose you leave work early on Saturday," I went on. "I hope your grandfather has not suffered from the wet weather."

"I believe he is very well," he replied.

I felt that our conversation was torture to him, and that he was merely enduring it by great effort of will. It was like holding a wild animal, which only waits till our grasp relaxes, and then bounds away to its hiding-place, henceforth to be shyer than

ever. I saw I should never get at him
through the ordinary avenues of neighbourhood and friendliness. To such entrance
his heart was closed. My only chance
lay in a sudden attack on some unexpected
corner.

" I should like to ask you a question," I
said, and was almost frightened to hear my
words.

His face changed colour and his lips
moved a little; yet there seemed a thaw in
his manner as he answered, " Very well, sir."

" I hear something is said against you in
the village. I have not heard what it is.
Will you tell me ?"

There was a long silence. We stood
just beside the fallen tree. I could see
some little boats on the silver breast of the
distant Mallowe, and thin smoke wreaths
rising from the house on its shore. I heard
a church clock strike four. My companion
stood motionless beside me, the outlines

of his face clearly chiselled against the pale blue sky—a handsome face, full of passionate sensibility, from which the old look of fierce endurance had fallen like a mask. At last he spoke : "They say I am a murderer!"

I did not shudder at the dreadful word, and somehow there was no query in my voice as I turned to him and said, "But it is not true."

"No, it isn't," he answered; "but it might be better for—for the others—if it were!"

"No, no," I said, "the more the sin the greater the sorrow."

"Well, I don't know," he went on in a choking voice. "If it had been found true, and I had suffered for it, every one would have pitied them; but as it is, they are only blamed and scoffed at for taking my part."

"But you don't suppose they mind that?" I inquired.

"If they don't, I do," he said.

"Sit down and tell me all about it," I said; "surely there must be some way out of this misery; tell it from the beginning, and take your own time over it," for I saw he was greatly excited.

We both sat down side by side on the fallen tree.

"It is a pity I was born," he said.

"Don't say that," I interrupted; "that might have saved your past, but it would also cost your future."

"My future!" he ejaculated, bitterly.

"Yes," I answered. "What do you call the future? If you measure it by the few fleeting years of mortality, you may as well style this field the world."

"I'm a living text for all the sermons in the neighbourhood, he broke out after a short silence. "There is not an idle reprobate in the place who does not set forth my ruin in excuse for not caring about his

children's education. I'm quoted as an instance of the folly of parents trying to elevate
their families above the station in which it
pleased God to place them. Every one is
sure I should have been a better man if I
had not known how to write or read. They
can't argue the subject, but they can point
to me in illustration."

At this moment it struck me that the
young man's whole manner was not that of
a country labourer. I had not noticed it
before, because my ordinary style of conversation is so homely that I need seldom lower
it for the simplest comprehension.

"Then your father brought you up care-
fully?" I remarked.

"Yes, indeed, he did," answered the
youth; "and he would have been angry if
any one had called us poor people, and I
was sent to the best school he could find.
But from the first there was something
wrong in me. The schoolmaster did not

like me, and I had not a friend among the boys. They knew who I was, and they did not care to receive me as an equal. When I discovered that, I turned it over in my mind, till I made out that according to their reckoning I was their superior: for however poor we were, I came of a nation the English could never subdue. They drove me to say so, and then they hated me, and I used to go to and fro with black bitter anger in my heart. Oh, what folly it all was! What folly!—if I'd known then what real trouble means—— Nevertheless," he went on, " I liked school for the sake of learning, and I believe I got on pretty well. But when I was fourteen my father died, and somebody got me a place in the builder's counting-house at Mallowe. The builder's son had been my schoolfellow, and the same week that I entered his father's shop he went to college. I suppose I envied him. I don't know how it came about, but I grew a very bad lad. There was something in me which would not be satisfied with my work and my home. Then Alice got a situation as lady's-maid, and grandfather went into lodgings, and there was nowhere for me to go of an evening. And yet it was not that either, for whenever grandfather called to see me I made some excuse to get rid of him, and when Alice wrote to me I seldom answered her letters. One of the young men in my master's shop was a Londoner, and he seemed to have so much more life in him than the others that I made friends with him at once. I got so fond of him that he could persuade me to anything. I used to go with him to all the cricket-matches and regattas within reach. Those things are harmless enough if one goes to them in good company. But poor George was not good company. And so I went on from bad to worse."

" Until——" I remarked, to lead him on, for he paused.

" Oh, the story is just like a common report out of a dirty newspaper," he said, writhing.

" Never mind that," I said; " and we should not call such things common if we only realized what anguish they each bring to somebody."

" Well, I got in debt to George. He gambled, and often had plenty of money. Then we grew quarrelsome. One Saturday afternoon last summer twelvemonth we went together to a boat-race. He drank a good deal, and betted and lost. I tried to get him away, but he only became very angry, and used violent words about the money I owed him. At last we left the place together. He had lodgings up here, and I meant to see him home. But he got so aggravating that my temper was roused, and I left him, and returned towards the

river. Just as I was passing the church I
saw Alice riding in her mistress's carriage,
and she looked from the window and recognised me. After taking a walk, I went back
to my master's house and slept there ; and
on Sunday morning we heard that George
was found drowned in the water in the
Low Meadow."

He spoke these last words in a low,
horrified tone. It was the first time he
had told the story. I did not break silence,
but waited till he resumed the narrative.

"I was arrested that evening," he went
on, "and I own everything was against me.
I was last seen with the dead man, and we
were heard to be on bad terms. One or
two people swore to seeing us together on
the road a good way from the river. One
man, an ostler, knew the exact time when
we passed his tavern. It was half-past
four. From that house it would take about
three-quarters of an hour to reach the Low

Meadow. I did not re-enter my master's house until half-past six, which allowed me full time to go the whole distance and return."

" But your sister had seen you in the interval," I remarked.

" Yes; and as she was driving past the church, she had happened to notice the time, and it was then about ten minutes to five. Her mistress remembered this, and also that Alice had nodded to some one on foot. That was all the evidence I could bring forward in my favour."

"Slender as it seems, it was sufficient," said I.

" It might have been if Alice were not my sister," he replied. " But every one is quite willing to believe that she swore falsely to save me."

" But her mistress partly corroborated her," I remarked.

" Not in the main point," he said. " The

lady knew that my sister nodded to some one as they passed the church at ten minutes to five; but she did not see *who* it was. So the coroner gave a verdict of ' found drowned,' and I was discharged, because 'there was not evidence whereon a jury could convict.' "

" But didn't they take into consideration the poor man's intoxication ?" I inquired.

" Yes : they consulted on the possibility of his slipping into the pool; but many swore that he was sober enough to take care of himself. I believe that was true."

" Then, what is your theory of his death ?" I asked.

" That he was murdered, or, at least, that a struggle took place on the bank which ended in his falling into the water. There were footprints of two people up to a certain point where the ground was much trampled, and after that there was only trace of one."

"It is very dreadful," I said; "and no one else has been arrested since your discharge?"

"No," he answered, hopelessly. "Suspicion did not point at any body but me, and so I must go through life as the murderer of the man who was my companion and destroyer. There is no appeal from suspicion!"

"Then you left your old service at Mallowe?" I asked.

"I was dismissed," he said, "and there was no chance of getting a similar situation. But I had been with my father a great deal when I was a boy, and so I am handy at any out-door work. But even that was not easy to get, till Mr. Herbert at the Great Farm took me on as a kind of general hand."

"There, at least, is a blessing," I said; "that saves you from being a burden to your grandfather and Alice, and——"

" I wouldn't have lived upon them while there was a rope in the house or water in the river !" he interrupted in the old desperate tone.

" What ! sooner than bear the weight of gratitude, you would plunge those who love you in despair?" I said. " I am sorry you are so selfish !"

He groaned aloud—" O, sir, have mercy on me. If you could only know how I feel——"

" Ah, that is it," I said, laying my hand on his arm. " If I only could ! But, my boy, God knows all about it, and He does not willingly afflict his poor children."

" But this false accusation—this wicked scandal—cannot come from God !" he exclaimed.

" He permits them—He does not wish them," I replied, recalling Ruth's remark. " No more did He wish a youth, the son of godly parents, to go with evil company, and fall into wicked ways. You must learn to pardon your neighbours' mistake. Your conduct has led them into this breach of charity. You have been to them an occasion of falling."

" And must the world always go on thus?" he cried.

" Remember, God over-rules all these troubles," I went on. " He saw you were proud and wilful, and He has been pleased to humble you, and to put your steps into straight and painful paths. He changes your neighbours' mistake into a merciful rod to correct you. You must not cry out at the rod, you must be thankful for it, and repent of the sins which brought it upon you."

" But the innocent suffer with the guilty," he said, raising his eyes. " *They* feel the rod as well as I do."

"That is part of your punishment," I answered. " But do not understand me

that affliction follows sin as a judgment. God
sends sorrow to draw us back to Him, or
nearer to Him, as the case may be. The
judgment of sin lies in our remorse for it,
and our grief at consequences which we
cannot undo. It is right you should smart
to see the troubles of your dear ones; but
yet those troubles may be a blessing to
them."

He had buried his face in his hands, and
I saw a tear trickle between his fingers.

"Your grandfather bears it very bravely,"
I said presently. "I daresay he thinks
little of any sacrifice which serves to steady
you."

"That's just what he says; but it's killing
Alice," he answered, without looking up.

"*You* are killing Alice," I said firmly.
"She cannot bear it because she sees that
you do not bear it cheerfully. Now, will
you not candidly own that you often speak
sharply to her?"

" Who told you so ?" he asked in astonishment.

" My own knowledge of human nature,"
I answered : " when she comes near you, the
sight of her recalls all the misery and bitterness, and doubtless you see she is whiter
and thinner than she was two years ago.
Then your heart rebels, and you ask yourself
grievous questions which you are not able
to answer, and meanwhile you forget the
smile and the pleasant word which would
send her away rejoicing. Next time she
comes back whiter and thinner than ever, and
the same weary work is done over again."

" But what am I to do ?" he said, looking
at me with eyes of such despair that I could
hardly confront them.

" Humble yourself, and leave the past
alone," I replied. " Remember that you
have sinned, and forget that you have been
sinned against. Draw your thoughts from
your injuries to your errors."

He sat in silence for some minutes, then the church clock chimed five, and he arose, suddenly.

" Then you believe I am an innocent man, sir?" he said.

" I do, sincerely," said I.

" I'll try to do as you say, sir," he remarked presently.

" You must excuse my plain speaking," I said ; " I don't often take folks by storm as I have taken you."

" I wasn't worth the trouble," said he.

" Don't forget you are worth a good deal to two or three people in the world," I answered, " and you'll set a value on yourself, some day soon."

He smiled sadly and shook his head, and so we parted, and I traced my way alone.

I had plenty to think about, in this grim common-place tragedy which had met me on the threshold of my retired life. I felt a warm interest in Ewen M'Callum. He had passed through a dreadful trial, but I could see it was just the trial he needed. Think of his schoolboy pride in belonging to a nation which had never been subdued! Ah, now he knows his own weakness, and one has to know that before one can be really strong.

Then I pondered over the mystery of the Low Meadow. Even Ewen concluded that his unhappy comrade had not met his death by mere misadventure. If this were true, the young man's character might yet be cleared by the discovery of the real criminal. But Ewen himself owned that suspicion had pointed to nobody but him, and surely the police would have tracked every possible clue they could find. It made me shudder to think that the murderer might yet be haunting the neighbourhood, not even aroused to confession by the danger and misery of an innocent person. Now, what would touch such a heart as that? I should say "nothing," only I know that God can do anything.

As I drew near home, there came through the open window a pleasant clatter of spoons and china. It was tea-time. In the hall I met Alice carrying the toast rack.

"I think you will find things get much better soon, Alice," I said, cheerfully.

She looked up at me with sudden brightness and asked: "Have you been speaking to Ewen, sir?"

"Yes; and I believe I have got into his heart," I replied.

"Did he mind—I mean how does he seem now, sir?"

"Well, Alice," I answered, smiling, "I think he is quite as well as can be expected after the operation."

Then we went into the parlour, and Alice deposited the rack on the table, and Ruth looked at her and then at me, and quite understood that I now knew all about it.

She is a wonderful quick woman, one of the sort that know things before they are told. I can never make out how she did not guess about Lucy Weston.

"So you've had your conversation with the young man," she said, as soon as the girls had left us.

"Yes," I answered; "and I have come to the conclusion that he is as innocent as I am."

"Why, surely you didn't talk to him of —what they say, Edward?" she exclaimed.

"Yes, I did," I replied. "I asked him to tell me all he could about it."

"Well, that's delightful simplicity!" said Ruth, laughing; "nevertheless, I believe simple people often do the wisest things. Let me put another lump of sugar in your tea, Ned."

"Thanks for your compliment," I said, holding up my cup for the proffered sweetness. "Don't you know, Ruth, that my

pet theory is the mission of Thorough-
fares ?"

"I want a report of that mission," said
she. "I don't quite understand its operations."

"Well," I answered, "when I was in the
city, "I used to notice that streets through
which no one could pass were always miserable. The houses got bad tenants, and the
bad tenants grew worse every day. I remember one instance in particular. It was
a long, narrow street, opening from a road
and ended by a dead wall. The houses near
the road were well enough. But as you
passed down the street you saw that each
dwelling was shabbier and dirtier than the
last, until close to the dead wall, you found
broken windows screened by torn shawls or
dirty blankets, through whose tatters you
could see family operations not usually
carried on in the eyes of the public. It
was a hopeless street,—a property so bad

that the landlord vainly advertised it for sale. But in the course of some improvements, the dead wall was pulled down, and the lower end of the street thrown open to a rising thoroughfare. And before a year was out, either the old tenants had departed, or they had mended their ways, for there was no untidy window or slatternly woman to be seen. Now I believe it is just the same with our hearts. Sin or sorrow sometimes close them so that no friendly voice can echo through. And gradually, all foul things congregate therein. Then some hand must break down the barriers with kindly violence, so that God's comfort may blow through like the healthy north wind which leaves a blessing behind it. And that makes suspicion and despair get ashamed of themselves and sneak out of sight, while love to God and man passes up and down the new thoroughfare."

"That's all true enough," said Ruth.

"But don't you think that in due time most hearts re-open without any interference?"

"Perhaps they may," I answered, "but they may remain closed too long for their own happiness or the good of the world."

"Yes, that's quite possible," said she, and she looked very grave. "But still, Edward, don't you think some sorrows are best endured and conquered in silence?"

"I do think so," I replied; "but then sorrow is not meant to close the heart, but to open it, and if we feel our heart closing, we may be sure we are neither enduring nor conquering, but succumbing."

There followed a long pause.

"A false accusation is a terrible thing," said Ruth, at last, "for it is very dreadful merely to be misunderstood."

"I don't believe you would mind even that," I remarked; "you are brave enough

to say, ' If God and my conscience approve,
let others think what they may.'"

"You are a wise man, Edward," said
Ruth, drily. Now what she meant by that,
I cannot tell. I am sure she did not mean
exactly what she said.

" It is to be hoped that you practise what
you preach," she added presently. "If you
have made a thoroughfare in this young
man's heart, make a thoroughfare in his life
as well."

"Please explain yourself, Ruth," I said.

" Why, don't you see he is cooped in a
corner," she answered, taking up her knit-
ting-needles, " with a lie behind him, and
the whole village in front, hunting him
back upon it? I suppose the world has
more places in it than Mallowe and Upper
Mallowe."

" Well, now I think of it, I wonder he
did not go abroad," I said.

" Yes, of course, brother," answered Ruth;

" because you know people can travel about so easily who have neither money, nor friends, nor character, particularly if they have aged or feeble relatives with whom it is their duty to stay. I must repeat, Edward, that you are a very wise man !"

"But if he went to London," I said, "then he wouldn't be too far from his grandfather and sister—certainly he might go to London."

"Certainly he will," said Ruth, "if you send him."

"But still, out-door work there would be worse than here," I remarked, "and, under the circumstances, other employment would be hard to get."

"Then never talk to me again about your city influence," said Ruth, knitting furiously.

"But, my dear," I pleaded, "we have only our own impressions to go by, and——"

"Edward," said she, laying down her

needles, and looking at me awfully, as she used in the days of my youth when I faltered in repeating 'my duty to my neighbour,' "Edward, do you believe this young man innocent, or do you believe him guilty?"

"I have no doubt of his innocence," I answered.

"Then do your duty according to your lights," said she; "that's all the best of us can do."

"But I could not recommend him to any one without telling him the whole story," I remarked.

"Certainly not; but I repeat, if you can not get anybody to share your convictions, or at least to trust them, I would not give much for your city influence."

"But would he be better off anywhere, when once his story was known?" I queried.

"I should think so. I presume a re-

spectable merchant could hear such a narrative without telling it over to all his clerks
and errand-boys. Were no confidences ever
placed in you, Edward?"

"Well, my dear, "I answered, "let us
call Alice, and if we can ascertain from her
that the scheme is likely to prove agreeable
to her brother, I will write to my old partners, and the youth's mind need not be
disturbed about the matter till we have a
definite offer to make him."

"There, that will do," said Ruth; and
she got up and rang the bell, and in half a
minute Alice's patient face appeared at the
doorway.

"Alice," I said, "come in; I have some
questions to ask about Ewen. We all
believe him innocent—my sister, you, and I
—but we fear it is very hard to defy a
general bad opinion. Do you think Ewen
likes remaining in the neighbourhood?"

"Oh, sir," exclaimed the maiden, wringing

her thin fingers, " do not set him thinking about going abroad !"

" Don't be a simpleton, Alice," said Ruth ; " now you are feeling for yourself instead of your brother."

"Hush, Ruth," I interrupted. " Alice is only nervous because she is weak and weary with sorrow. I am not speaking of abroad. I think it is a great blessing that he could get honest work close at hand, for Mr. Herbert had as much reason as other people to mistrust him. By the way, I wonder that did not help to re-establish Ewen's character, Alice."

" It could not, sir," she answered. " Every one knows that Mr. Herbert would not care if he were guilty, so as he could get him cheap."

" Now, I fear that is rather uncharitable, Alice," said I.

" It may not be so, Edward," remarked Ruth. " ' Charity thinketh no evil,' that is to say, she does not suspect, but she cannot shut her eyes to facts."

"I am not ungrateful to Mr. Herbert, sir," said Alice. "His work has been a blessing to us, for the other gentlemen round here would not hire Ewen at any price."

"Well, what I wish to ask is, do you think your brother would be better off in London? Take time to consider. There are many questions to answer. Has he had sufficient warning to steady him? Can you and his grandfather bear to part from him?"

"Oh, sir," said Alice, with streaming eyes, "if he could get work more fit for him than field-labour, and be out of sight of all the people that shun and scorn him, grandfather and I wouldn't think about ourselves."

"Now I believe you love your brother," remarked Ruth, quietly. But the girl dropped her head and wept bitterly.

" I suppose he would have no objection to any plan of this sort ?" I said presently.

" He would bless you and thank God for it, sir," sobbed my servant.

" Then don't repeat our conversation at present, and I will see what can be done. Trust me, he shall not be left in his present misery if I can help it."

" Though he must not forget it is principally his own fault," said Ruth, parenthetically.

" And now you may go, Alice ; and you may tell Phillis to get supper ready."

" No, I'll tell her myself," interrupted Ruth ; " and if Alice likes, she can go straight off to bed, else Phillis will think she has had a very bad scolding."

" I don't care what any one thinks, ma'am," said Alice, joyfully, though the tears were still streaming down her cheeks.

"Now, isn't that extraordinary?" remarked Ruth, when she was gone.

"That in particular?" I inquired.

"That girl's love for a brother who has never made her happy. People who are wicked, or useless, or unlucky, seem always the most thought of."

"I suppose it is a provision of God," I said. "He longs to save them from themselves. If we stood on shore and beheld a shipwreck, we should throw out most ropes to those who could not swim."

"But still it seems hard," said Ruth.

"Well, so it did to the prodigal's brother," I answered; "but depend upon it, when they both sat down at the family feast he was the happier of the two; or at any rate, he would have been, had he loved his brother as he ought. You see, he might have watched at the gate beside his father, and then he would have been better employed than weighing and measuring affection, and disturbing himself with reproachful thoughts."

"Ah, yes, so he would," said Ruth; "of course I know God in his wisdom manages these things best; and that just shows us how foolish we must be; for if we had the reins we should do almost everything differently."

"And yet, Ruth, I believe no fiction ever points so clear a moral as one life lived fairly through," I observed, "and that is how God sees every life from its beginning. We only read one or two chapters out of each history: or if we happen to see nearly all, we do not possess the key, which would show us a hidden meaning."

"I suppose it is so," said she, folding up her knitting; then, with a change of tone, she continued, "but if I were you, Edward, I would write that city letter directly, so that it may go off by the next post."

I wrote it, and when it was signed, sealed, and stamped, my vigilant sister was satisfied, and we had our supper and went to bed in peace.

I did not go to sleep directly, for my room
was glorious with moonlight. I lay still
and pondered over the events of the day;
and most of all, I mused over the depths of
sin and suffering that might lie hidden
behind the calm smiling front of such a
tiny village as Upper Mallowe. When I
passed Mr. M'Callum and Ewen in front of
Mr. Herbert's farm on the day of my arrival,
how little I dreamed of the tragedies in
which they were both called to bear part!
And so it often is. We read of saints and
heroes, of martyrs and sorely-tried folks, and
then we go out into the world, and marvel
why we meet nothing of the sort. All our
own fault! We cannot see the romance
because our eyes are too weak to pierce its
common-place vulgar wrappings.

"Just like a common report in a dirty
newspaper," said poor Ewen of his sad story.
And yet if we move the scene from an
obscure village to a great capital, and change

the persons from unknown working people to princes and generals, this is the stuff of which much history is made. We are all so taken with the glitter and grandeur, that many who would shudder to come in personal contact with " common " crime like this, are ready to spend years in writing the defence of some royal " suspect," long dead and gone beyond the reach of calumny or justice. But I suppose my mind is not strong enough to love great heights and long distances. I would rather confine my interest to the little world lying close round me. I always find that it contains far more than I can manage, and I should often be quite disheartened if I did not remember that our Saviour approved her who just " did what she could."

Then I fell asleep. And when I awoke the room was bright with sunshine, and I heard a low sweet voice softly singing——

" Praise God from whom all blessings flow :
Praise Him, all creatures here below ;
Praise Him above, ye heavenly host ;
Praise Father, Son, and Holy Ghost."

For a moment I forgot forty years ; but when I remembered all about it I felt no pain, for I know Lucy is still singing in our Father's upper chamber; and next to the sweetness of a dear voice, is the sweetness of a voice which we have made joyful.

Alice was the singer.

CHAPTER III.

ST. CROSS.

"What are your household arrangements for Sunday, Ruth?" I enquired of my sister when I joined her at the breakfast-table.

"Why, of course, you and I go to church, Edward, and so does one of the girls, and in the evening I shall stay at home, and they can both go out."

"Shall you send them to church?"

Ruth shook her head. "I haven't hired their souls as well as their bodies," she said. "I never speak about such things to my servants until I am their friend. Because a girl is in domestic service, why should we conclude that she is naturally disinclined to her duty, and must be preached and driven into it?"

"But as a mistress, you have a right—" I began.

"To set a good example, as far as I can, to give them time and means for self-improvement, and to encourage them to do right by not suspecting them of doing wrong," interrupted my sister. "And, by the way, Edward, what 'rights' did you exercise 'as a master' over your clerks? Not many, I expect, and I'd rather follow your practice than your precepts."

The parish church of St. Cross was not very far from our house. As we approached it, its appearance did not gladden my heart. It stood in the angle of a small green, flanked by a few straggling houses of the meaner sort. In the midst of the green was a wide pool of sluggish water, inhabited by a colony of ducks. The church itself was a long low edifice of no particular order of architecture, with an insignificant spire, and a single dismal bell, more like a signal for an execution than the summons to God's house. Around lay a little graveyard, wherein most of the graves were covered down with huge flat stones, which, not to be blasphemous, always suggest the idea that the survivors had resolved to do their utmost to prevent a resurrection. Up to the porch, between these gloomy tombs, ran a narrow path of rough sharp stones. Certainly that path would never tempt any shoeless wanderer. The porch itself was narrow, and the inner doors were closed and guarded by an injured-looking female in a widow's cap. I paused in the porch and looked round—and I pitied the little children who would remember that church as the place where they first went up to worship God.

Passing through the folding doors, which opened with a dismal creak, we found our-

selves in a passage-like interior, lit by narrow windows filled with opaque glass. Now,
I dislike opaque glass even in city churches,
for I think a ragged back wall is better than
a blank, and I don't see why a cat, peace-
ably creeping along a coping need disturb
the sanctity of any congregation. But
opaque glass to shut out green trees and
open sky! With a shudder, I turned to the
pew which the disconsolate widow opened
for us. It was not far from the pulpit, and
was snugly cushioned and carpeted. I did
not discover the narrowness of the seat until
I had risen from my knees, and was, I
trust, in a more contented and devout frame
of mind.

Then I looked towards the communion
table, hoping to find some comfort there,
but I only saw bare white walls, relieved by
two tablets whereon were written the ten
precepts of the law. The table itself was
small and high, and grudgingly covered with

shabby crimson velvet, edged with tarnished gilt fringe. On it stood two straight candle-sticks. But above all rose the single adornment of the building—a painted window representing the Descent from the Cross. The colours were laid on so thickly and darkly that the picture was only illuminated round the central figure—the dead body of our Saviour, gaunt and wrenched, half-wrapped in blood-smeared cloths. The painting suggested no idea but that of fearful physical pain and exhaustion. I think angels veiled their faces before the reality of the scene. Why should we hold it up for our children to gaze upon while they weary of the sermon, and long for the Sunday pudding? It was frightful!

Slowly the congregation gathered in. I saw Alice and her grandfather, but not Ewen; I saw other faces which I had seen pass my gate, but with which I could not yet connect any idea. But just as the bell gave its last lugubrious stroke the bereaved attendant bustled up the aisle with increased alacrity, followed by the brisk step of a middle-aged gentleman. I recognised his bronzed face and beetling brows : it was my nearest neighbour, Mr. Herbert, of the Great Farm.

Close at his side walked a young lady, dressed very quietly in grey mantle and bonnet trimmed with purple and black. They both entered the great square pew immediately in front of ours, evidently *the* pew of the church, with seats on all sides, and an oaken desk in the middle. When I caught sight of her face, in the midst of that dreary building, it came to my mind like a line of poetry quoted in a dry theological tract.

Yet it was not a beautiful face. I do not suppose an artist would have been satisfied with one feature. I think its charm must have been that the veil of flesh was so delicate and frail that the soul shone clearly through—a sensitive, shivering soul, which would need a very warm mantle of love to pass safely through this chilly blustering world. There was nothing about the face which will stand description, except perhaps the dark hazel eyes, very intense and bright, yet with a look that somehow suggested they had often glistened through tears.

She gave just one glance towards us, and then stood up and opened her book to join in the service. For by this time the clergyman had entered.

He was a young man, with plain features, and resolute, sensible bearing. I knew his name was the Reverend Lewis Marten. And the clear, distinct tone of his voice was the first thing in the whole church which gave me unmingled satisfaction. But when we kneeled down for the Confession of Sin, imagine my horror to find that we were expected to go through it in an undefined chant, rendered absolutely ludicrous by an attempt to join, on the part of some old people on the free seats. And I found the same thing went on whenever the congregation should respond. I never say a word against cathedral-services—they have trained choirs, and audiences, as a whole, highly educated. But can the same arguments be used for little churches, dependent on a singing-class or charity schools, and where the main object should be to render the whole service intelligible and profitable to such as cannot read, or have no book? I don't suppose God's word has any exact precept for or against such performances, but does not St. Paul say, " All things are lawful, but all things are not expedient?" And he uses some other arguments which wonderfully suit these customs when viewed from another aspect. I should like to hear what the Reverend Lewis Marten thinks of the 14th chapter of Romans.

We got through the prayers, and through an anthem which was not in our hymn-book. It was performed only by the schools and a few giggling boys in a pew behind the reading-desk. While this went on, Ruth kept her seat, with that awful expression of countenance which I know means a great deal of anger, with a strong spice of contempt. I stood up, for I don't think such a matter is worth a breach of the peace. I only think it a great pity—a very great pity!

My hopes revived when the young clergyman mounted the pulpit in his black gown. His face was so rational and open, so free from the covert humility of priestcraft, that I felt sure his ideas were not so mediæval as his customs. I was right. But still I was disappointed. Everything he said was true, but it was only half the truth. He spoke of the sin of our hearts, the utter emptiness of the world, and he garnished his discourse with pithy aphorisms, and flashy poetry. But scriptural words of healing and comfort were not set therein, like "apples of gold in pictures of silver." He showed us the suffering without the salvation,—Golgotha without the Saviour who died thereon. And the old men and women fell asleep, the charity boys "swopped" their marbles, the singers giggled and whispered, and the dark eyes of Mr. Herbert's companion turned ever and again to the fearful picture above the altar. And I could not help being glad when it was over, and so I am sure was the preacher.

When I turned to leave, I found the church had been but thinly attended, and that the majority of those present belonged to the classes which have but a loose hold on the stirring interests of life,—young boys and girls, aged people, and those miserable-looking objects who haunt the regions of clerical almsgiving. Now that is a view of religion, which I can never understand. To me, it seems that it should have the strongest claim on those who are in the front rank of the battle, that they should find God's house verily a house of refuge, wherein to rest and recruit their strength for each new campaign. And I am sure there is something wrong in the religion which fails in this. By my own heart, I could trace how the declension might proceed. Next Sunday morning, if it were wet, or if I were weary, it might seem to me more profitable to remain at home with my Bible and good books, than to attend a service that chilled and disheartened me. And thus, a church-going habit once broken, I might get so accustomed to my good books, that I might long for a change, and take to essays and history and so on, till at last I might fall to the depth of newspapers and gossip. And thus it may have been with the honest yeomen and buxom matrons who left their empty seats before God in the church of St. Cross.

In the pebbly graveyard we overtook our Alice, with her grandfather leaning on her arm. I thought I should like a little talk with the old man, for his face had been the best lesson of the morning,—a sermon beaming with the comfortable truth that one may be very old, and very poor, and very tired, and yet very happy.

"What, Mr. M'Callum," I said, stepping to his side, "are you a deserter from the kirk?"

"Na, na, sir," he answered with his blithe smile, "I'm just a sheep that's been carried frae its ain field, and must e'en pasture where it can; and, praised be God, there's grass growin' everywhere."

"Is there no Scotch church within an easy distance?" I asked.

"Na, sir," he said; "the nearest is full fifteen mile frae this. Aince on a time, I

made shift to get there every Communion
Sunday—which was four times a year. But
noo-a-days I go but aince, so that I'm
broucht back to the privileges o' my young
days. For ye see, sir, we lived in a country
parish, and only gathered for the Lord's
Supper just after the harvest was in."

"I daresay you wish there was a Scotch
church close at hand?" I said.

"Aweel, sir, of course, there's nae kirk
like the auld kirk, to my mind; but still
there's a poo'er o' grace an' glory i' the
Church o' England,—the twa are sisters
like, sir, only the ane is a sonsie gudewife,
in her braw white mutch, and the ither is a
grand princess in her jewels. They fall out
a bit sometimes, as sisters will, but there's
the same heart i' them baith, sir, and they've
but ae Father."

"I am sorry to see St. Cross has not a
larger congregation," I remarked.

"The people hereaway don't go much to

church, sir," he said : " I've aften talked tae
them about it. Ye see, I'm an auld man,
and I've come frae sic a far-awa' place, that
may be they're mair patient wi' me than if
I was a poor body that had ne'er been
ayont the parish. I tell them about the
shootin' grunds, and the moors, and the deer-
stalkin', and they're glad to listen, and then
after a bit, I can bring the talk roond—ye
understand, sir."

" And what do they say about neglecting
church ?" I inquired.

" Some say it's a dour place, and gies
them the miserables ; and some say parson
doesna tell them anything new, only that
the world's a wicked hole, which they ken
well enough already ; and some canna stand
the chantin'."

" And no wonder !" ejaculated Ruth.

" Aweel, mem," he went on, turning to
my sister, " I think it some queer myself,
mair especially as I canna hear what they

say, and I'm ow're blind noo to read the
biggest print. Hoo the honest Church o'
England should want to mak' herself look a
bit like the Lady of Babylon, is what I canna
understand. But still, I aye say to mysel',
if ane gies up the kirk, he gies up
Sunday, and then the days rin on without
sense or meaning, like print wi' the stops
no put in. Anything's better than that."

"Has Mr. Marten been clergyman here
long?" asked Ruth.

The old man shook his head. "It
seems but the other day he came, mem
but time passes quickly. How long is it,
Alice?"

"Just two years, grandfather," she answered.

"Aye, aye, just two years," repeated he.
" I remember, I remember, Alice. I think
he's a good young man; he was verra kind
to us when—aye, you know now, sir! Only
he thinks a college education maks mair

difference than it does, sir. He's feared it
keeps folk frae understanding him. And he
looks at things in a gloomy way; but that's
aften the case wi' young folk. Life comes
unco hard tae them at first, puir things,"
and the old man glanced at his grand-
daughter.

"Ah, by the way, Alice," I said, "I've a
letter in my pocket that you may as well
drop into the post now, for I should like it
to go off the first thing to-morrow morning," and I handed her the epistle bearing
the London address. It caught her eye,
and she smiled brightly as she hastened
down the turning leading to the post-office,
whilst we and her grandfather waited at the
corner.

"Your granddaughter seems a blessing to
you Mr. M'Callum," I said.

"Aye, she is that; and so is the
boy, poor fellow — he'll be a brichter
blessin' some day. Thank you kindly

for your goodness to him yesterday, sir."

"What! did he tell you of the talk we had?" I asked.

"Yes; he seemed main thouchtfu' all the evenin', and yet he wasna sad or sullen. An' at supper time, he said, 'There's some one else thinks I'm innocent, grandfather,' and then he told me all about it."

" Does he never come to church?" inquired Ruth.

"He hasna come regular for a long time—and never since *then*, mem," answered the old man. "Ye see, the folk would hardly have sat in the same aisle wi' him! But he seemed inclined to come this mornin', and I hope he'll mak' up his mind to be there the nicht; he'll tak' courage i' the dusk, may be.

"If Alice would like to pass the day with you, we will spare her," said my sister, as the girl rejoined us. "Phillis can manage to-day, and Alice must do as much for her in a Sunday or two."

Alice looked up into my sister's shrewd, brown face, and she let that look be all her answer, leaving the audible thanks to her grandfather.   And so we parted.

" That was very kind of you, Ruth," I said, as we went on alone.

" May it not be their last Sunday together?" she answered.   " Don't you think I know how a woman feels before a parting? —the more fool she, for a man never cares !"

That is Ruth's way of speaking, whenever she is caught doing a kindness.   And it is astonishing how she always brings in something complimentary to the male sex.   And the worst of it is, sometimes I can't say these compliments are unmerited.   So I generally let her take the field, whilst I retire into the nearest ditch.

"I'm afraid you don't like St. Cross?"
I said presently.

"Like it?" she said, with bitterness.
"Edward, I've endured it four Sundays,
and I wouldn't allow myself to say a word
to you about it, because I wanted you to
see it with unprejudiced eyes. But it drives
me mad! If I could get at these boy-
singers in their white gowns, wouldn't I
find out whether they know their catechism!
And I'll engage they don't! What can a
clergyman think about to put a parcel of
lads into a seat together, instead of each
of them sitting beside his own father and
mother, and learning to behave in a reverent, godly manner?"

"It seems a mistake," I said; "but no
doubt Mr. Marten does it in hopes of ren-
dering the service attractive."

"Attractive!" she answered; "if any
one wants such attractions, why do they
put up with shams? Why don't they go

where they can get the reality—to the Church of Rome?"

"But the sin of the Church of Rome is not so much her ritual as her doctrine," I pleaded, rather wildly.

"Don't the two go together?" said she. "I wonder the Israelites didn't plead that it was only 'harmless ritual' when they danced round the golden calf! Perhaps Aaron meant it so."

"But, my dear Ruth, the innovations at St. Cross are very few and faint," I expostulated.

"They're are as much as they can be," she answered grimly. "There's a choir in white, and they and Mr. Marten all turn to the east two or three times in the prayers, and every response is chanted, and there are candlesticks on the communion table. Anything more would cost money, and the church doesn't look as if it had any to spare."

"These things seem to me so pitifully trivial as to be beneath mention," I said.

"Is it wisdom to overlook the egg until the serpent is hatched?" she asked.

"Mr. Marten has a pleasant, sensible face," I remarked, "and there is something I regret much more than these petty ceremonials, and that is, the cold, repellant tone of his sermon. I should like a little talk with him. He is a young man, and a glimpse of an old man's experience can do him no harm."

"It would be less trouble to build a new church at once," said Ruth, cynically.

But that is just like her. I hope for the best, and she prepares for the worst.

As we entered our house, it struck me painfully, that instead of returning with God's peace on our hearts and tongues, we had come back in a criticising, flaw-detecting spirit.

And what seemed worse, I could not conclude it was altogether our own fault. I resolved, however, that Ruth's hopelessness should not dishearten me. I must try to do good in my own way, and I am always inclined to mend rather than remake. So in the course of the afternoon I startled my sister by announcing that I should write to our young rector, and invite him to spend an evening with us in the course of the following week.

"It is his place to call upon us," said she.

"Certainly, Ruth, and doubtless he will do so; but you see I do not care about a call, I want a long friendly visit."

"Then I wish I could go to tea somewhere, and leave you to fight out your battle by yourselves," she remarked.

"There will be no battle, Ruth," I

responded. "I only want to ask him the general position of affairs in the parish, and how I can best make myself useful."

"Then he will say they want a new altar-cloth—not to say a new organ—and also more funds that the choir may be enlarged," said she.

"Well, I'll tell you what the church does want, Ruth," I answered, "and that is, new windows. It is a sin that thick glass should come between us and the blue sky."

"What, let in more light to the candles on the communion table?" queried Ruth, sarcastically.

"The candles are not lit," I said.

"But I suppose they will be some day," she returned. "They are not there for nothing, surely."

"Perhaps the sunshine will put them out, Ruth," I said.

" I hope it may !" she retorted, grimly.

I did not answer, but opened my desk, and began to indite my letter to the clergyman.

" Won't you help me, Ruth?" I asked, after putting down the date.

" It is quite your business," she replied. But the dear woman is far too active-minded not to interfere in anything when asked. So presently she said, " You may send my compliments, I suppose. And what do you mean to say, Edward?"

" Will this do?" I asked her, and read:—

" Mr. and Miss Garrett present their compliments to the Rev. Lewis Marten, and hope he will do them the honour of spending an evening with them in the course of the week. Mr. Garrett is anxious to get acquainted with the neighbourhood, and trusts that Mr. Marten will be

willing to advise how he may become
useful therein."

"I suppose that will do," commented
Ruth; "and yet, brother, the fact is, you
want to advise *him!*"

"I don't deny that, but it is quite true
I wish information which he can give."

Ruth looked at me for a moment and
then her grave face broke into a smile.

"Any one would say I managed you,
Edward, but I doubt if I do," said she. "I
think you know how to get your own way
without making a struggle. But, by the
way, I don't like letter-writing on Sunday."

"Why, this is only an act of neighbourly
kindness!" I said, surprised. "We are
always free to do good on that day."

"Certainly, Edward; and yet I think we
should keep up every possible distinction
between the Sabbath and other days."

"You don't think the day of rest should
be a day of idleness, Ruth?" I asked.

"No," she answered; "but I think with Mr. M'Callum that Sundays should be the 'stops' in our life. I know some people laugh at Scotch notions of Sabbath-keeping, but that is because they never tried the refreshment afforded by the day, when life stands still before the throne of God, and care and weariness are swallowed up in His glory."

"But, Ruth, may it not be that while we try to keep the letter of the positive law, we are in danger of neglecting some moral duty?" I inquired.

She shook her head. "I don't think so. The very day of rest helps to discipline the mind to distinguish between what it wants to do, and what it should do. If a letter would prevent a mistake, or save an hour's unhappiness or give comfort, I should say, write it—aye, and carry it yourself, though the task occupied your whole Sunday. I was glad to see you give that letter to Alice

this morning. But what will do quite
as well on Monday, leave till Monday,
and certainly this note can wait till to-
morrow."

I felt that Ruth was right. And I put
away my desk.

CHAPTER IV.

THE RECTOR'S VISIT.

THERE was rain on Sunday night, and when we looked from our windows on Monday morning, we found but a dreary prospect. Many leaves had fallen, and lay sodden and decaying in the garden path, and the few remaining flowers looked as if they only lingered to bid us a last good-bye. A light mist hung over the scene, and shut out the distant meadows. Ruth ordered fires to be lighted, and advised Alice to put on a warm shawl when she went to carry my letter to the rector. Winter never finds my sister unprepared, and perhaps there is no instance in which forethought saves more health, comfort, and good temper.

Alice returned in due time, saying she met the rector at his gate, and he detained her while he read my missive and penned his reply, which proved a very courteous one, stating he would have great pleasure in waiting upon us that very evening.

Five o'clock found Ruth and me seated opposite each other, with the lamp on the table between us—I lingering over the pages of a monthly periodical, and she busy with a huge bagfull of gay scraps, by which I understood that patchwork was on hand.

"Phillis is a terrible blunderer with her needle," said she; "she shall not live in the house with me, and not learn better. Patchwork is good practice, and as the quilts get made, I can give them away to the old people round."

"I fear they need blankets more than quilts," I ventured to say.

"Very likely. That is your concern," she

answered, coolly. "Money buys blankets, and you are a rich man. But if you were bedridden, Edward, you would know the comfort of a bright quilt to cover the fuzzy blanket. And patchwork is quite a fortune in a house with a sick child. Do you remember ours at home?—the silk quilt which mother used to show us on holidays." And when I glanced at my sister, some minutes after, her face was still soft and tender with the recollection of the faded finery.

Every day, sitting opposite Ruth, I am struck with the exceeding beauty of good old age. In youth, my sister was plain, her features harsh, and her figure and movements too decided for grace. But Time has dealt with her like a patient artist with his picture ; so that she is a noble old lady with a grand brown face, crowned with white hair, and lit up by eyes which have not forgotten to flash and sparkle.

Presently the gate clanged, and in a

moment Phillis ushered in the clergyman, who brought with him the peculiar damp, chill atmosphere of an autumn evening. I think he was glad of the welcome offered by our cheerful fire, and he seated himself on a chair indicated by Ruth, and rubbed his hands in the genial warmth. They had no fires yet where he lodged, he said. He had not noticed the deficiency until he saw ours, but he remembered he had been very cold while studying. He must speak about it to-morrow.

And so we kept up a good-humoured chatter till tea was brought in; and when we were fairly established round the table, with cheering cups before us and a pleasant prospect of tea and toast, Ruth inquired if St. Cross were a comfortable church in winter.

"I regret to say it is never comfortable," replied Mr. Martin; "in summer it is close and dark, and in winter cold and damp."

"Yet it is well situate," I said. "The

darkness is only due to the narrowness of the windows and their thick glass."

"You are right, sir," he answered. "And why a church should be so built I cannot understand."

"Nor I," I said. "To shut God's light from God's house seems to me worse than foolish. Why do you not remedy it?"

The young man looked at me, and smiled grimly. "Neither my predecessor nor I have been able to muster more funds than barely suffice for whitewashing and cleaning," he replied. "The parish is not rich, and the people do not seem liberal. At the present moment, the church is absolutely falling out of repair. We have had one or two collections in its behalf, but the money comes so slowly that I fear the building will be in ruins before the requisite sum is made up."

"Why don't you repair first, and collect afterwards?" I asked.

"Sir!" exclaimed the young man in astonishment.

"Yes," I said, "why don't you get some kind friend's promise to make good the deficit—if any?"

The rector shook his head. "I wish we had such a friend in Upper Mallowe," he said.

"Are you sure you have not? Have you asked every one?" I inquired.

"There is no one to ask," he answered, adding suddenly—"unless it be you!"

Ruth laughed outright.

"I should not wonder if it were me," I said.

"My dear sir, I did not expect this," said the young clergyman, very radiantly indeed.

"You need not thank me, Mr. Marten, until you see whether I have any balance to pay," I observed.

"Ah, I know you will," he replied,

shaking his head. " I know my parishioners. You are a stranger among
us, sir."

" We shall see who judges them best,"
said I.

" My brother is always hopeful," remarked Ruth; " but I must say he is
generally right."

" We must not attempt any serious re-
pairs until spring," I said, " but in the
meantime cannot we make some little tem-
porary improvements? I observe that the
old people sit about in cold parts of the
church, where, if they be at all deaf, they
cannot hear a word. Why don't you give
them those comfortable seats round the
reading-desk ?"

" They are kept for the choir, sir,"
answered Mr. Marten, reflectively.

" Excuse me," I said, gently, " but in
many churches, and certainly in St. Cross,
I think a formal choir is a mistake."

"So do I," returned the young man frankly, and Ruth gave an unmistakeable look of pleasure. "It was established by my predecessor, who thought otherwise. I found it when I came, and I have not abolished it because I dread meddling with existing arrangements, and because I fear to deprive our services of what is generally considered an attraction, lest our small congregation should become still smaller. Many people believe they derive benefit from the full carrying out of the ritual of the Anglican Church."

Here Ruth broke in. "They like fine singing and pretty altars. If the ritual be performed shabbily, they don't care for it. Since I have lived in this parish I have learned that many of your young people walk to Hopleigh, five miles off, because the church has a splendid choir and enticing decorations. Unless you can afford the same, your ritual will never secure them,

though it may drive away people better
worth keeping."

"I do not belong to the High Church
party," said the young rector, quite humbly,
"and I am always sorry that St. Cross
wears the badges of the same. But
what can I substitute for the choir?
We have no charity-school on which to
depend."

"Of whom do the choir consist?" I
asked.

"Of the sons of farmers and tradesmen
in the parish," he replied. "They meet
for practice twice every week—after the
Wednesday evening service, and on Saturday night."

"You don't have them in a Bible class,
then?" queried Ruth.

"I have nowhere to receive them,"
answered Mr. Marten, dismally. "If they
came to my lodgings the landlady would
complain of their wearing out her carpets,

and our parish school-room—I dare say you saw our little school in the aisle—the parish school-room is such a rookery that their parents would think it an insult if they were invited there."

" A good opportunity to hint they should build a better one," put in Ruth.

Mr. Marten smiled, and shook his head in resigned despair concerning the efficacy of such hints.

" Can't you have them in the vestry ?" asked my sister.

" Why so I can !" he exclaimed. " It's rather small, but it will do. I wonder I never thought of that !"

" Where there's a will there's a way," said Ruth.

The young clergyman blushed slightly.

" Mr. Marten must pardon us," I said, " we are getting old," (" We are old," said Ruth,) " and we forget sometimes that we have no parental rights over young people.

We are only anxious to do a little good before we go away."

"And old people can seldom do better than set the young ones to work," observed Ruth. "I only made the suggestion because I thought the class would keep them together, and they might go on with their practising; and I think they would sing better standing decently at their mother's side than now, when they are always ready to burst into a giggle."

"Ah, I'm afraid they behave very badly sometimes," sighed the rector. "But as the stoves will be lighted next Sunday, I will take the opportunity to direct that the old people shall sit round the desk and enjoy the warmth, and I must manage about the boys as well as I can."

"Mr. Marten," said Ruth, "you cannot tell how glad I am that it is only a matter of 'management.' I feared we should have to fight out a battle about apostolic succession, and an infallible Church, not to say the Real Presence, and other dogmas."

"Ah, Ruth," I observed, "if Mr. Marten were the staunchest advocate of these doctrines, I should not attack them; I should only say—'Think of the old people, and do not keep them in the cold —remember the people who can't read, and don't sing to them'"—(and I glanced at our guest, in hopes he would take a hint from my words). "Differences of opinion will never be reconciled by argument, but any sect will shrink from confessing that its theories will not let it work under Christ's great banner of 'Love to the brethren.'"

"I do not adhere to one High Church doctrine," said the young rector; "but yet I cannot help thinking some of their innovations are improvements."

"Certainly," I responded. "For instance, I like the idea of free churches : the rich and the poor equal before God."

"I don't," said Ruth. "The rich and poor are equal before God ; and no arrangement of seats can make any difference. You look at it from the wealthy point of view, and you like to flatter your spiritual pride by a semblance of self-abasement. Some people seem to think the poor are only made to practise their virtues upon, particularly humility, like the cardinals at Rome when they wash the beggars' feet. But just view it from the other side. Would not you rather sit among your own people— the pensioner and the farm-labourer and the servant-girl together—than flourish your rough hands and poor, coarse clothes among the silks and velvets of the gentry ? There are two sides to every question; but I always think it is best to let people stay in their own places, just because I believe that in God's sight one place in the world is quite as good as another, and that the labourer's horny hand is as honourable as the prime minister's worn brow. But their outward conditions can never be the same till they're both in heaven. And if they be wise men, and recognise their true equality, they will not wish it otherwise."

"Very likely you are right," responded the rector. "Viewed in that light, probably the poor, as a rule, are happiest among the poor. But dropping the subject of free seats, I am sure you would not wish to check honourable ambition. One is often struck with a great disparity between the mind and the position."

"Certainly," said Ruth, with a humorous twinkle in her eyes. "I knew a man who blamed statesmen, and censured clergy, and had splendid ideas of what he could do in their place, whilst his own home was in disorder, and one or two of his children might have given him valuable information about prisons and workhouses. There was a great disparity between his mind and his circumstances, only it was the wrong way!"

"Oh, Miss Garrett, you refuse to understand me!" cried Mr. Marten, smiling. "I mean that a great mind is sometimes found in a lowly place, and surely you would not wish such to remain in the position wherein he was born."

"He'll often wish himself there before he dies," answered Ruth. "He'll find God gives hard work in the upper classes of His school. But he's sure to be promoted, not because he was too great to do the easy tasks, but because he was great enough to do them well. God wastes nothing, Mr. Marten. If he make a genius, He has got something for him to do besides breaking stones; but most likely He will keep him doing that, till by virtue of the power that is in him he does it better than

any one else. Don't you remember it
s said when Shakespeare got his living
by holding horses, he did it so well and
was in such demand, that other men hired
themselves under him, that they might call
themselves 'Will Shakespeare's lads?'"

"But still many geniuses are sad failures
in the ordinary walks of life," remarked Mr.
Marten.

"Ah, those are poor, unhealthy geniuses,
who slip from God's grasp into the devil's,"
answered Ruth. "They let go their Father's
hand; but I think He generally catches
them against their will; only they get so
torn to pieces in the struggle that the best
work they can do for Him is the warning of
their example."

"Still, there remain a few sad cases which
cannot be classed under any rule," said the
clergyman, thoughtfully: "Chatterton, for
instance."   .

"Yes, poor Chatterton!" replied my sister

in a tone so different from her own that I
looked up. " Almost every writer has said
something fine about Chatterton : heaps of
sentimental pity, with a spice of blame for
his wrong-headedness, or recklessness, or
want of faith, which they seem to think
brought down his miseries in punishment.
Not one thoroughly realizes that he was
only a boy—a child, and that none of his
faults and blunders need be wondered at. It
was his time for being checked and chidden,
and comforted afterwards. But he was
dropped upon the world with no one to screen
his follies until they were corrected. If he
had only known a little love——"

" I always understood his mother and
sisters——" began Mr. Marten.

" His mother and sisters must have been
weak, shallow women," interrupted Ruth.
" They believed all his poor, fine stories !
Love gives the greatest fool more wisdom
than that. All you men blame Horace

Walpole. So do I; but I blame those women more. That boy had lived with them sixteen years, and they did not understand him. It was a noble wish to keep all his struggles to himself, but it was cowardly in them to allow it. I can't believe they thought everything right; God help them if they did, for the revelation came too late."

"They were very poor, and doubtless ignorant of the world," pleaded Mr. Marten; "but the whole story is sad and mysterious, like a psalm of humanity with the love of God left out."

There was a pause.

"But the misery is," added Ruth, suddenly stirring the fire, "that the same thing may be going on somewhere at this moment, and we don't know."

"God can do without our help," I said, softly, "if He does not show us where to give it."

And then followed a long silence, which I broke at last by asking the rector if he knew much of the M'Callums.

"I saw a good deal of them about eighteen months ago, when they were in some difficulty," he replied; "but I have not called upon them lately. The old man is very kindly, and the grand-daughter—your servant, Miss Garrett—struck me as a good girl. But the young man is as ill-conditioned and morose a fellow as I ever knew. Their trouble was about him, and I fear there is little doubt he was guilty of the crime imputed to him. He avoided me as much as possible, but I ventured to speak to him once, saying I hoped he would be warned of the wickedness and danger of neglecting his religious duties and consorting with evil company, and he turned and answered me in a terrible way—a terrible way, Mr. Garrett."

"What did he say?" asked Ruth.

"His manner so astonished me that I can scarcely recall his words," returned the rector; "but it was to the effect that it was not his fault if some bad people were more attractive than some good ones, and that he guessed, in my day, I had done as much as he to deserve suspicion."

"Dreadful, dreadful!" said Ruth; but she smiled as she said it.

Mr. Marten looked aggrieved, and turned towards me. "I had only spoken the truth with the authority of a clergyman," he observed.

"Why didn't you try speaking the truth 'in love'?" I asked; "that is St. Paul's counsel."

"I certainly did not speak it in malice," he replied.

"Should you have said the same thing to your brother, had you such a relation in Ewen's place?" inquired my sister.

"Well, not exactly," confessed the rector

—" circumstances make things so different."

" Mr. Marten," I said, " will you take a hint from an old man, who has lived in the world more than twice as long as you ?"

" Not one hint, but twenty," responded the young man, cordially.

" It is this. Never address the vilest outcast as you would not speak to your dearest friend. Even were this young man the criminal you think him, you and he have the mutual ground of a common humanity. The gentleman-parson should not have lectured the peasant, but the man in you should have spoken to the man in him."

„ You are right, sir," said the rector, heartily, " I accept your reproof ;" and he took my hand and shook it, adding, " and I only wish th young man had shown himself wiser than me, by taking my blunder in

a more kindly spirit, for it is not pleasant
to recall his answer."

"Yet there was truth in it," I observed,
"and he did not mean it for the insult it
seemed. He declares himself innocent of
the murder, and conscious of this, he felt
the sting of your implied suspicion, and
retorted with the conjecture that, in your
days at school and college, you had perhaps
fallen into many misdemeanours, such as
those he confesses, and which your wiser
guardians regarded as the foibles of youth,
but which in his case exaggerating gossips
blacken into confirmed bad character."

"I can understand that," said Mr. Marten,
reflectively.

"Ewen was wrong to speak so," I went
on; "but I fear he was almost in despair.
The gentlest animal will turn upon its
pursuers when it sees no way of escape. He
cannot justify himself further than he has
done, and his tormented soul was ready

to take shelter behind the mask of ruffian-ism. And if that mask be worn too long, Mr. Marten, it is rather hard to throw aside."

"You speak as if you believed his innocence, sir?" observed the rector.

"So I do," I answered. "I noticed something strange in his manner, and I heard dark whispers concerning him. So I asked him to tell me all about it. And he did not omit one shadow from the gloomy picture. I believe he is as innocent as you or I."

"Then I feel as if I could go and beg his pardon directly," said the rector.

"That's right," said Ruth; "we shan't make mistakes in the next world, so this is our time to practise penitence."

"He was with his sister at last evening's service," remarked Mr. Marten. "I dare say he came because his heart was touched by your kindness. He sat in a lonely corner in the shadow. And when I noticed him, I thought, 'That reprobate has come to God's house because it is too damp to wander in the fields.'"

"And if it had been so, what did it matter?" observed Ruth. "If God drives a man into church by wet weather or a snow-storm, all you've got to do is to say something which will make him come again."

"Oh, dear, I am so sorry!" bewailed the young man; "I feel as if I should never be uncharitable again."

"Oh yes, you will," answered Ruth, "and be sorry afterwards, I hope. That's about the best we can do, from the cradle to the grave."

"It is always safe to hope for the best, Mr. Marten," said I.

"So long as you prepare for the worst," put in Ruth.

"I dare say I have often done harm where I have tried to do good," said the rector, ruefully. "I am so lonely in this dull country-parish, that my mind gets sour and jaundiced. I am inclined to envy my brethren whose lots are cast in London. They have earnest work to keep their souls healthy. If they wear out, that is better than rusting out."

" Whoever can't work here, couldn't work in London," answered Ruth, decisively. "If a man is not strong enough to walk to his own gate, he needn't wish to climb moun-tains."

" Now, for my part," I said, " I think a country clergyman is a very happily placed man. His work is ready for him, and it is not more than he can do, if he go about it honestly and heartily. He is surrounded by means of healthy relaxation, in the proper use of which he can set a good example. He is known and honoured everywhere, and he knows and cares for everybody. His education and knowledge of mankind enable him to widen the narrow

village life, and connect it with the busy
world beyond. Sometimes he can help his
city brother, for the restless tide of labour
often throws a few wanderers on his quiet
shore, and he has it in his power to link
some holy memory with their recollections
of his fields and farms. That is my portrait
of your life, Mr. Marten."

"It is so flattering that I do not recognise it," said he, with a smile—rather a
melancholy one.

There was a pause, for Ruth sat lost in
thought. Suddenly she roused herself, and
asked, "Have you a refuge in the village,
sir?"

"No, ma'am," answered the rector. "If
belated travellers cannot pay for a bed, we
inhospitably refer them to the workhouse at
Hopleigh. If they die on the road—they
have done so once or twice—there is an
inquest, and the Union buries them. That
is our English version of the Good

Samaritan.   It is useless to disguise the truth."

"Then let us try to make it truth no longer," I said.   "I know you will have an earnest helper in Ruth, for refuges are her favourite form of charity."

" Because, if they be well managed, they do so much good at so little cost, and in such a kindly way," she remarked. "If we give hungry men a tract on the goodness of God, need we wonder if they throw it away with a curse. A meal and a bed would preach a far better sermon."

"Certainly, if their hearts were sufficiently open to receive it," said Mr. Marten, dubiously.

"There must be something to put them in mind," replied my sister, "but I don't believe many people are so hardened as you think. Anything roughly knocked about gets battered and black outside, but the tough rind may keep something very soft within."

"I shall be only too happy if you will help me to try the experiment," said the rector; "my heart has often ached to see the poor creatures starting on their long journey to the tender mercies of the Casual Ward."

"Aye, you may well say 'tender mercies'!" responded Ruth; I am quite astonished to find, that as a rule, workhouse chaplains think they have no duty to discharge towards these strays. They don't want preaching. But surely they might go in and commend the great family to Him who remembers every one of them. That would comfort some, and a good word can't harm the worst. And in the morning I think the chaplain might go again, and see if any one wanted advice. A little counsel is sometimes worth more than a fortune. If the chaplains can't do it, I wish some one else could get permission."

"It will take us some time to get a refuge organised," remarked Mr. Marten, presently.

"We only want a six-roomed cottage, no matter how rough or old-fashioned—the more so the better; it will be more like home," replied my sister; "and then we must get a nice, comfortable couple, to live in it, and act host and hostess. And, of course, you must persuade all the village to help us, Mr. Marten."

"O dear, dear!" said the rector, despairingly.

"Never venture, never have," I observed.

"I will help you. I believe I am a good beggar."

"You have let them lose the habit of giving," said Ruth. "Like everything else, it grows easier by practice, sir."

"Well, Miss Garrett," he said, rising, "I must thank you for originating so excellent a plan. I shall mark to-day with a red letter, in commemoration of this visit, and in a few days, I dare say, I shall bring you word of suitable premises."

He would not stay to supper: so, after a little more talk about the best ways and means to further our plan, Ruth and I escorted him to the door. The ground was still damp, but there was a pleasant drying breeze, which made me long for a little ramble under the starry sky. So I proposed to walk home with our guest. Ruth expostulated, but I put on my great-coat, and had my own way.

The clergyman lived down the road, past the Great Farm, and as we walked we chatted cheerfully about divers things, and it gratified me to believe that the

young man was in better spirits for his
visit to us old people. I know some
of Ruth's words were very sharp, but
so are mountain breezes, and yet they
do us good. They make us turn about
and look at things under different as-
pects, and that is a healthier proceeding
than standing still, peering through our
own little glasses, which perhaps are
yellow !

We turned the corner occupied by the
Great Farm, and presently the sound of
hurried footsteps warned us of a wayfarer
advancing towards us. In a moment he
came up.

There were no lamps on the road, and I
could only distinguish a tall figure, muffled
in a cloak, and a face which looked very
pale in the moonlight. He was walking
rapidly, but the rector turned and watched
his form as it swiftly receded into total
darkness.

"Surely that is young Herbert," said Mr. Marten, half aloud; "and what can he be doing here?"

I remembered the name of the family at the Farm, and concluding this individual to be one of them, nothing seemed more natural than his presence close to his own home. And so I silently wondered at my companion's wonder.

We parted at the rector's gate, and he detained me a moment to congratulate me on having such a sister as Ruth.

"Her society is like a draught of quinine," he said.

"Ah," I replied, "her words have bristles on their backs, but we all want brushing up sometimes!"

"I hope she won't spare me," he said; and I think he was sincere.

"Never fear," I answered. "Good-night."

But as I walked back, I wondered what made my sister so terribly earnest about Chatterton.

CHAPTER V.

TURNED TO THE WALL.

On Thursday there came to me a letter bearing the London postmark. I saw Alice look at it as she took it from the postman and she brought it into the parlour and laid it on the breakfast-table with its super-scription upwards. I recognised the writing of the kindest man in my old firm, and I had little fear about its contents, so I bade my servant wait a moment.

The epistle was short enough. The "house" regretted that my first recommen-dation was not a case which they could take up with more zeal. But they would stretch a point to oblige me. So, if the young man liked, he could take a subordinate place in

their counting-house at a salary of eighteen
shillings a week.

Now, I did not read the letter to Alice.
I knew it was very kind, but to her it
would seem cruel. I only told her the
result of my application. She took it very
quietly, with a few grave thanks, spoken
slowly and laboriously, like words in a
half-known tongue, ending with the request
that she might go and tell Ewen.

I reflected for a moment, and then said,
"No, I should like to speak with Mr. Herbert first; he has been kind to your brother,
and I should not wish to entice him from
his service without his knowledge. I will
make everything right, and your brother
shall have the offer before the afternoon."

And Alice thanked me again, and went
away to the kitchen.

I wanted Ruth to accompany me to
the Great Farm, but she refused, saying
I suited strangers better than she did, and

she hated morning calls. I learned afterwards that she and Alice passed the time in consulting over the outfit necessary for the lad's decent appearance in his new situation.

I saw neither Ewen nor his grandfather on the way to the Farm. I proceeded to the dwelling-house, and found the garden gate open. The bad weather had made sad havoc among the shapely flower-beds, but a few chrysanthemums smiled from the withered leaves, like country faces in a London crowd. So I reached the broad old-fashioned porch, and pulled a bell whose handle I found among the ivy leaves.

The door was opened by a middle-aged woman, tall and gaunt, clad in a dark clinging gown, and thick white cap and apron. She might have been portress at a nunnery.

"Is Mr. Herbert within?" I inquired.

"Mr. Herbert has just gone out among

his fields," she answered, in a sour tone, eyeing me like one who has reason to suspect a stranger.

"Can you tell me where I may overtake him?" I asked.

"H'm—ye see he's moving about; and as you went in at one gate, he might go out at the other. I don't know whether he'll be long. If ye'll step inside I'll just inquire."

She admitted me into a square wainscotted hall, pushed forward a heavy oaken chair, and retreated with noisy steps through an arched doorway.

The place reminded me of dear old Meadow Farm, only on a grander scale. There was the same wide fire-place, surmounted by hunting trophies and blunderbusses, the same bare walls and floor, only these were of oak instead of deal. But it was very silent, and there was no cheerful family litter on the hall table—no whips, or dog-collars, or battered gardening-hats. I had scarcely time to notice all this, when the tall servant returned.

"Will ye just step into the parlour to Miss Herbert?" she said, and turned about and led the way. She had never asked my name. It seemed that unexpected visits were so rare in that house that she had forgotten the customary etiquette of such occasions.

The "parlour" was reached by a short passage leading from the arched doorway. This passage was very dark, and as my guide opened the door at the end, I was almost dazzled by the sunlight in the white-ceiled and delicately-papered room beyond. The servant made way for my entrance, but did not retire.

Miss Herbert advanced to meet me. As I expected, she was the lady whom I had seen on the previous Sunday, but in her in-door apparel she looked much younger.

She met me close to the door, and her face seemed anxious and fearful. There was a dog at her feet, a curly honest-eyed fellow, but not such a one as usually frequents feminine boudoirs.

" I apologise for disturbing you," I said ; " but I wish a little conversation with Mr. Herbert. I must introduce myself as Mr. Edward Garrett, your new neighbour."

"Oh, indeed !" she responded, in a relieved tone, " will you please take a chair ? I expect Mr. Herbert will return in half an hour. If you can wait, he will be very happy to see you."

Then she resumed her seat, and the attendant, who had remained till now, closed the door and left us together. Like all English people, we entered into a conversation about the weather, from which we passed to the scenery in the neighbourhood, and similar topics. On Sunday, my companion's face

had awakened my interest, and as we talked
this interest deepened. Her manner was
refined and kindly, and her smile was that
beautiful smile which suggests a burst of
sunshine on a rainy day. Yet there was a
pre-occupation about her, as if her thoughts
perpetually slipped away elsewhere, and had
to be forcibly recalled and kept at their duty.
As we talked, there came upon her face the
anxious laborious expression sometimes seen
in deaf people, and then she spoke with a
fitful, forced vivacity, as if she feared she
was failing in her part, and threw out all
her energy to succeed. Altogether she was
exactly the reverse of the calm, healthy
woman one expects to meet in a farm-house
parlour.

"I hope your papa is not so busy this
morning that I shall be troublesome,"
I remarked, after one of our very natural
pauses.

"Oh, no," she answered, rousing herself

with a start; "but Mr. Herbert is not my father : he is my uncle."

"I beg pardon for the mistake," I said. "Then are you one of the household here, or are you on a visit?"

"I have lived here since my father's death three years ago," she replied. "Up till that time I was with him in London."

"Ah, so we shall be able to talk about the great city," I said. "But I dare say you do not know much of the part most familiar to me—eastward of Temple Bar."

"Oh yes, I do," she answered. "My father was a literary man, and we went about a good deal."

"A literary man." I knew that means such different careers—a refined retirement graced by many of the comforts and privileges of rank and wealth without their restraints and responsibilities, or a hurrying life in restless homes, shiftless labour, improvident speculation. Perhaps this was the key to the overwrought face before me.

"Which do you prefer, town or country?" I asked.

She shook her head. "I can't say—one may be happy in both, or miserable in either."

"Then, at least you do not dislike rural solitude?" I remarked.

"I was always accustomed to solitude," she answered. "Mamma died years ago, and I was an only child, and my father was generally much engaged."

"Ah, then you may be less lonely in a family house among the fields than in rooms overlooking London streets," I observed.

She smiled faintly, and did not reply. Presently she rose and said we had best find our way to the dining-room, as her uncle sometimes came in by a side-door, and sat there looking over his papers, long before any one knew he had returned from his rambles.

"I am sorry to give so much trouble," I apologised, as I followed her guidance; "my business is only a little matter about one of the farm people. If I could see young Mr. Herbert——"

We were crossing the hall when I said this. She stopped short, looked up at me, and repeated my last words. Surely it must have been the effect of some stained glass above the door, but her face looked scared and white.

"Have I made another mistake?" I queried. "Is there no young Mr. Herbert? I fancied so, because I was out with a friend a few evenings back, and I thought he called a gentleman by that name. Such are the difficulties of introducing oneself, Miss Herbert."

God forgive us for the pain we unintentionally give! She moved forward again,

and led the way down another short passage.
As she paused to open a door, she turned
and said in a very soft, low voice—" We
are a small family at the Great Farm—only
my uncle and I."

The room into which she ushered me was
a long, low, wainscotted chamber, with a
window at either end, one opening into the
garden and the other into the conservatory.
The furniture consisted of highbacked, red-
cushioned chairs, two or three carved chests,
and a table spread with a white cloth, and
sundry preparations for lunch. The walls
were enlivened by a few heavily-framed
portraits in oils. Now, I always take interest
in family pictures, but as I glanced over
these, I saw something which gave me a
sudden chill.

It was nothing dreadful. Household
skeletons are generally shut in very common-
place cupboards. There is no unpleasantness
in the back of a canvas when we scan it

in hopes of finding some clue to its pedigree. But it brings an awful revelation of domestic agony when, in a pleasant family room, we come upon a picture TURNED TO THE WALL.

Miss Herbert made no effort to renew our conversation. She drew a chair towards the fireplace, in mute invitation for me to be seated, and then went to the conservatory and began gathering dead leaves into a little basket. It occurred to me that she had brought me to that room expressly that I might understand there was delicate ground in her uncle's dwelling, and so be warned to tread warily.

In a few minutes the master of the house came in, and greeted me very cordially. Now he knew me as a respectable neighbour—not as an unknown lounger peering over his hedges. But it's an ill compliment to be suspected till one's credentials are shown.

"Come, Agnes," he called to his niece, "come and take your place at the table, and

do the honours. Rather a young housekeeper, you see, Mr. Garrett, but as discreet
as if she were fifty," he added, as the young
lady obeyed, with a pale ghost of a smile
flitting over her face.

I would have excused myself from his
bluff hospitality, pleading "that I would
not detain him five minutes, I only wished
to speak about a little business——"

" And what business on earth is not better
for being discussed over ale and ham ?" he
answered. So I had no alternative but to
accept a chair and a plate.

"You have in your service a young
man named Ewen M'Callum," I began very
primly.

"Ah, that I have," said the farmer.
" And there isn't a better workman in the
place—can turn his hand to anything.
Good job for me that he's rather under
a cloud, else he would not be hired for my
price."

"Then, Mr. Herbert," I responded, "I fear you will not thank me for asking you to give him up?"

"What! do you want him yourself?" he asked. "Upon my word, you city gentlemen are keen in detecting the value of a good article."

"No, I don't want him myself," I answered; "but I dare say you know the youth has capabilities rather above farmwork."

"Certainly I do," said he, "and that's just the reason why he's so good at it. Everything's the better when done with brains. I only wish they would get so cheap as to be included in engagements."

"I have succeeded in getting him a place in the city—something of the kind he had before he——before he passed under the cloud, as you say," I explained.

Mr. Herbert's face clouded, and he asked

very shortly, "Does the young fellow know this?"

"Not yet," I replied. "I would not name the subject to him, until I had conferred with you."

"That's right," he said, clearing up. "'Pastors and masters,' and all that, you know. We must stand up for it, sir. The young ones are always ready to throw us over. Well, let 'em if they can. If they won't have our rule, they can't want our help."

Now, I felt that Mr. Herbert spoke truth, and yet I could not assent. It pains me to hear truth spoken dogmatically or maliciously, or selfishly, and though the farmer's seemed only a coarse, good-humoured, give-and-take selfishness, nevertheless it profaned what it touched. But he did not notice my silence.

"I'll not stand in the lad's light," he went on. "We'll go out together, and we shall find him somewhere about, and then you can tell him, and he shall have his wages, and a bit over, may be. He's been worth double the money he's cost; but, of course, I shan't say so. He's a civil lad, too, though he's short-spoken, and doesn't say two words, if one will do."

"He will be all the better when he is out of the way of suspicion," I said.

"I don't see why he need care for suspicion," responded Mr. Herbert, with a contemptuous emphasis on the word, "except that it lost him a good place. But anything else might have done that. Suspicion can't hang a man, and so far as I can see, it doesn't hinder his enjoying any comforts he can get."

"But a man does not live only to eat and to escape the gallows," I remarked. "That's a dog's life, Mr. Herbert."

"Let who can live for better things," he said, recklessly. "Let 'em have fine hopes and visions, they'll find 'em less substantial than this," and he slapped the ham with his carving-knife.

"Certainly, sir," I answered, "just as the perishing body is, to our gross senses, more substantial than the immortal soul."

Mr. Herbert made no reply, but helped himself to some ale, and told his niece she ate no more than a chicken, and there was a silence, until I inquired if Miss Herbert's London training permitted her to be a good walker.

"Oh yes," she answered, with that same aroused manner. "I think nothing of what many women call long distances."

"But you hardly ever go out, now, Aggie," said the farmer, in a softened, kindly tone.

"I wonder at that," I remarked, "for I know there are beautiful walks about here, and I am sure you must have plenty of leisure."

"Yes, plenty of leisure," she repeated absently.

"Can you sketch?" I inquired.

"I used to do so," she answered.

"Now, how interesting that would be," I said, "for you might bring all the beauties of the neighbourhood into your uncle's house to brighten a rainy day."

She laughed a little, and then answered, "There was nobody to see them. Uncle would not care," and I thought she glanced towards that picture with its face turned away.

"But anyhow it would occupy your time very pleasantly," I went on. "Don't the days seem long to you, alone in this house among the fields?"

"Oh, the days pass somehow," she replied, with such a short, sad laugh.

"I wish she would not shut herself

up," said Mr. Herbert, uneasily. "She's always willing to go out if I ask her, but she never proposes it of her own accord."

"Then, sir," I said, "I wish you would now ask her to accompany me to see my sister. Ruth will be very glad to have a young thing about her as often as the young thing likes." But even as I uttered the words I felt that my sister, with her white hair, was far less weary and worn than this twenty-year-old girl. Agnes Herbert's sweet tired face positively pained me.

"Then Agnes must be at her service," said the farmer promptly. "So, my girl, go and put on your wraps, and you can come with us through the fields. The walk will do you good, this fine sunshiny day."

She rose to obey, smiling and silent. It was the silence about her which was so pitiful. For silence is the leaden shield

with which we meet the inevitable. Hopelessness is silent. So is Death.

She was ready in a few minutes, and we
three started from the back-door —" the
field way," as Mr. Herbert called it. He
was quite eager to show me every object of
interest, and I don't for one moment suppose that he identified me as the Cockney
traveller whom he had half anathematized
for peering at his crops. Agnes stood beside us, while we discussed sundry items
of agriculture, and she answered when ad-
dressed, but when left alone, I don't think
she listened. However, when the conversation passed to haymakers, and similar
" odd hands," and I remarked that we hoped
to establish a little village refuge, which
might be useful to such, or to others in dis-
tress, she suddenly looked up into my face,
and said—

" That will be very good."

" Aye, so it will," observed her uncle ;

"they can put up there on days when we farmers don't want them, and then they'll be at hand when we do."

"I shall ask you to subscribe, Mr. Herbert," I said.

"Well, I'll give something—it will save me bribing 'em to hang about idle,—picking and stealing."

"And you too, Miss Agnes?" I queried.

"I have so little money," she answered.

"Then Ruth must find out how else you can help us," I remarked.

"I'll thank her if she does," said Mr. Herbert. "Aggie sat and looked at the fire all last winter, and all this summer she has looked at the grass. Anything will be better than that—whether it does good to others or no."

So we walked on through meadow after meadow, yet we did not find Ewen, but only his grandfather, who told us the young man was "away in the cart." I announced my proposal to the patriarch, who received it with very eager gratitude. "It will be the making of the lad, not that he ever said a word against his work; but it's no the richt sort for him—ye'll grant that, sir?"—to Mr. Herbert.

"I'll not grant anything of the kind," returned the farmer, with his bluff laugh; "but every man must stand up for himself, and I don't blame your boy for following his fortune."

"Ye'll no think him ungratefu'," said Mr. M'Callum. "He'll ne'er forget that wantin' your kindness he couldna hae bided here till the bricht turn came. He'll aye remember that, sir."

"There's nothing to remember," said Mr. Herbert; "I had a chance of a good workman cheap, and I took it. Tell him he can go away whenever he likes, M'Callum; he need not wait to give me proper notice. And you can hand him that from me," and he slipped something into the old man's hand, "just a kind of farewell blessing, you understand."

"Ewen will be prood, prood, if he can e'er serve you or yours, sir," returned Mr. M'Callum; but the farmer waved off his thanks and strode on, calling on us to follow.

"I'm called a 'near' man, Mr. Garrett," he said presently. "So I am. I wouldn't give a man high wages for the world. Bad principle. Keep 'em in their place. Make it up in presents. High wages make 'em independent in their service. Presents bind 'em to it. High wages set all the labourers round plaguing their masters for the same. Presents only make 'em anxious to get to the master who gives them."

"But, Mr. Herbert, is it *just* to give a man less than he is worth, and then bestow his own upon him as a boon?" I asked.

"Justice is an excellent lady, sir," he

answered, jocularly, " only she's blind, and there's no knowing where she'll lead one She has taken some people so far that they think it's sinful for one to be rich and another poor. They may go on till they find out that some have no right to be tall while others are short."

" That is mistaken indeed," I said ; " but the rich have no right to grind the poor because they are poor ; and in a crowd a tall man looks none the shorter for letting a little one stand in front."

" Ah, right enough," assented my companion. " 'Live and let live, is a good motto. But when you stand aside to let another pass, I like him to notice that you needn't do so if you don't choose."

" Then you are very fond of power, Mr. Herbert," I remarked.

" Indeed I am," he answered, candidly. " And if any one under my control is sensible enough to understand me, he can get pretty much his own way; but if he flies in my face and rebels—well—as I said before, I don't govern him, and I don't help him, that's all."

"But then you throw away the much stronger influence which patient forbearance would win," I observed.

He looked a little blank, but he only gave a whistle and stopped short, saying that he must turn back, and would send for Agnes in the course of the evening. So he shook hands with me, and sent his respects to my sister, and Miss Herbert and I proceeded to our house.

My sister received the young lady very kindly. I saw she noticed how girlish and transparent the fair face looked when the lace bonnet was removed. But she only rattled on in her sweet, old-fashioned hospitality, calling Miss Herbert's attention to sundry quaint knick-knacks scattered about our parlour, and giving their little histories. Our visitor merely answered "yes" and "no;" but she listened in the grave, pondering way of those who strive to bring every new idea to bear upon some old problem. After dinner Ruth let the conversation flag, and Miss Herbert did not take it up, but leaned back in the easy-chair, and seemed quite satisfied with the silence. As her uncle had said, she sat and looked at the fire, and I will confess that I sat opposite and looked at her. Gradually twilight stole over us, and as I watched her with half-dozing eyes, I became conscious of one of those strange revelations which come to us at such times, when out of the familiar face grows another face, different and yet the same, sometimes showing how the old man looked when he was young, sometimes prophesying how the boy will look when he is old. And lo! the hopeless face before me grew calm and firm, but no longer girlish, and the peace thereon seemed not of the simplicity which looks up at life's struggle, but rather of the wisdom which looks down upon the same. But the spell of my dreamy gaze was suddenly broken by Phillis bringing in the lamp, and Ruth rousing herself from the sofa behind me, and saying she guessed Miss Herbert would think us a fine set of sleepy-heads.

So the fire was stirred and tea ordered. Alice brought it in, and when she left the room Miss Herbert made her first spontaneous remark—

"That is Alice M'Callum, is it not?" she said. "She looks happier than she has looked for a long while."

"I dare say you know she has been in great trouble," observed Ruth; "but, thank God, there is no sorrow so dark that it cannot be lightened in God's good time."

"If it be God's will," Miss Herbert whispered, softly.

"And I think it is always God's will," answered my sister, in a clear, cheerful voice. "Sometimes He chooses not to take away our cross, but it is our fault if He do not help us to carry it, and when once He does that, the worst is over."

And I saw Miss Herbert paused, and let those words print themselves on her mind.

"Let us hope that in every sense the worst is over for Alice," I observed.

"Alice has never lacked blessings," returned Ruth. "Her troubles have not wasted her life, but rather ennobled it. Her calamities have compelled her to work harder than before, and more for other people than herself. All sorrow should lead to that, only it's a great blessing when we're put between two hedges, and so can't mistake the meaning of the signpost."

"Yet it seems to me that those who have done most for the world have been happy people," remarked Miss Herbert.

"Certainly," said my sister, "just because those who do good cannot be miserable. If we make smiling faces round us, we learn the habit of smiles."

Just then there came a gentle tap at the door, and Alice's face appeared, very bright, indeed, as she said, "Ewen has come up, if you please, sir, because he would like to thank you."

"Show him in," answered my sister.

The young man entered, and his sister retired. He was not in his farm clothes, but in such dress as he must have worn in the office at Mallowe—a suit probably never used since that time. He was a tall, well-made fellow, and I was glad he would certainly make a good first impression on my city friends, and I noticed that Miss Herbert looked at him with surprised interest. Naturally enough, he spoke shyly

and stiffly.   He was evidently very glad of
the impending change, yet in the gladness
was a reservation which he seemed unwilling
to express.   It came out at last.   "Grandfather will be so lonely."

"Ah, we must see about that. For the
first few days Alice can stay with him, and
come to her work here while he is out,"
answered my sister.   "And after that, some
new plan may suggest itself.   Does Mr.
M'Callum speak of it?"

"Oh no, ma'am," replied Ewen ; "for that
matter, I've been such bad company that he
won't miss me much."

"Have you seen Mr. Herbert?" I
asked.

"Yes, sir; I happened to meet him in
the road. He was very kind," with a glance
at our guest.

"Well, Ewen, you are the first person I
have recommended to my old firm," I said,
"so you must get me a good name for in-

sight and discretion, just for the sake of those who may come after. Do you know any one in London?"

"Not a soul!" he answered, with the gaiety of one who is not sorry for oblivion.

"Then take care what friends you make," I responded. "There are one or two Scotchmen in the office, to whom your nationality will serve as introduction. And for the matter of evening recreation—I know you are well-educated—have you any favourite pursuit—chemistry, or anything?"

Ewen smiled and blushed a little, and then answered, "I always had a taste for drawing, sir."

"Oh yes, I know," exclaimed Agnes Herbert, and checked herself.

"Then go to a drawing-class as soon as you can afford it; and even before that, there are many free evening lectures and exhibitions by which you can improve yourself. An inclination for any study is the cheapest and best pleasure a man can have. Pursuing it, he gains insight into other things, and is thrown in the way of congenial company. But don't let your taste run away with you; don't let it intrude on business, or sleep, or exercise. Don't allow yourself to be an indifferent clerk, for sake of being an indifferent artist. Be thorough in your duties, and you will elevate the standard of your taste."

"And don't forget to be regular in your letters home," said Ruth, practically. "Let them be expected on certain days, so that Alice need not waste her time waiting for the postman."

"And write to me whenever you like," I added as the young man rose to depart. "But I suppose we shall see you again before you go."

"I don't think so, sir," he answered. "Alice and I have talked it over, and she says I can be ready to go by the train to-morrow morning, and she'll send the rest of my things after me."

" You are indeed glad to get away, my boy," I said, as we shook hands.

" I'll not deny it, sir," he replied, " but please God I'll win to such a life that those who believe that black chapter will be willing to forget it."

" And is there no one else to whom you should say good-bye?" I asked. " A journey is none the worse for a few ' God-speeds.' "

" Well, there is one," he said, reflectively ; " but I was once so rude to him that I don't like to go. I mean our minister, sir."

" Go by all means," said Ruth, smiling. "You own you were rude to him ; so if you get a rebuff, it will only serve you right."

" Ewen," I interrupted, " if you go, take my word for it, you won't get a rebuff."

"I'll go," he said. "I'll go before I return home." And so he shook hands with Ruth and me, and was going away with a bow to Miss Herbert; but that young lady sprang up briskly and shook hands too.

"One of Nature's gentlemen," I remarked, when he was gone.

"A brave, honest man," said Ruth.

"You think him innocent?" queried our visitor.

"That we do," answered Ruth.

"Supposing he were guilty?" said Miss Herbert again.

"Then as he asserts his innocence, he would be very base indeed," returned my sister.

"I think him innocent," observed the young lady after a pause. "I always thought so."

"Did you express that opinion whenever you could?" asked Ruth.

"I said so to my uncle; but he did not

care, whether or no ; and I don't speak to any
one else."

"Then you should," answered Ruth, decidedly ; "we should all keep a seat for ourselves in the parliament of public opinion.
A single vote may turn the scale sometimes."

"But I am so fond of solitude," pleaded
the girl; "yet still," she added, eagerly,
"I would make myself like society if I
could do good in it. But if I had gone to
all the village tea-parties, and lifted up my
voice for Ewen's innocence, I could not have
helped him as you and your brother have,
Miss Garrett."

"Certainly not," returned Ruth, "your
time for that has not come. Youth is the
season for gaining a place and a voice in the
world. Influence is like everything worth
having : we must work a long while to
gain it."

"Well, Ruth," I said, "Miss Herbert has
her uncle's permission to help you about

your refuge.   That will be a beginning for her.   I think she is like you—in favour of refuges."

" Is that so, my dear ?" asked Ruth.

" Yes," answered the girl, very softly indeed ; " because they give one more chance to the lost ones."

" There are none ' lost ' between earth and heaven," said my sister ; " wherever they go they can't get away from God. And He gives them chance after chance to the very end."

" But He is angry with the wicked," whispered Agnes Herbert, with dilating eyes.

" Just as a loving father is angry with his naughty children," returned my sister. " He loves them none the less for His anger. He is angry because He loves them.   Like a father, too, He waits to forgive."

" But some fathers are not ready to forgive," said Agnes.

"Then they need to ask their children's pardon for their hard-heartedness," replied Ruth; "and God help them to see the necessity before it be too late!"

There followed a short silence, which Miss Herbert broke by the abrupt inquiry,—

"Do you think many people go to heaven, Miss Garrett?"

"Surely many more than go elsewhere," answered Ruth, "for God's love is stronger than Satan's malice. And heaven is broader than our charity. There will be some there whom we scarcely expect. Ah, it would be a woeful world if we could not always hope that!"

At this the strange, reserved girl suddenly sprang up, and kissed my sister with the bursting enthusiasm of one who has just heard unexpected tidings of joy. She would have subsided as suddenly, but my sister held her for a moment, and kissed that sensitive forehead—once, twice, thrice.

Agnes' impulsive embrace was like the electric shock which flashes across the sea the glad news that two nations have but one heart.

Here Phillis entered with the announcement that Miss Herbert was fetched, and that the rector's servant had brought a letter, which she handed to my sister, who presently passed it to me; and while Agnes put on her bonnet, I read aloud :—" The Rev. Lewis Marten sends his best regards to Miss Garrett, and he has found a house which he thinks exactly suits her ideas of a refuge. If convenient, he will wait upon her to-morrow morning, and take her to see it. He must add that he has named the subject to some of his parishioners, and has secured one or two donations; which is very promising."

" Would you like to join us?" inquired Ruth of Miss Herbert. " Come over here early, and take the walk with us. Remember, I shall quite expect you."

"Tell your uncle, and then he will take care to send you," I said, smiling. And so the matter was settled.

"A very sweet girl," remarked Ruth, when our visitor had departed. "At first I thought her listless. I don't think so now. And she has an energetic face."

"She seems like one defeated," I said, "who has no heart to recommence the battle."

"Then we must get her into it unawares," returned Ruth.

And I told her all I had seen and heard at the Great Farm about the girl's loneliness and her uncle's evident solicitude, and about the strange shadow of household tragedy that haunted the family dining-room.

"Doubtless she will tell us about it in due time," said Ruth, meditatively. "In the little intercourse I have had with people round, I have heard nothing about the Herberts. Very likely Alice could explain it. But she is not the girl to tell, and we are not the people to ask her. Whatever it be, they had better have taken the picture down and put it out of sight. Turned to the wall, indeed! What folly!"

CHAPTER VI.

MR. MARTEN PREACHES AT SOMEBODY.

THE next day we accompanied our pastor to see the proposed Refuge, and Miss Herbert did not fail to join us. The meeting between her and the clergyman was quite of the civil, distant order—so much so, that I wondered if the young man's exercise of his ministerial functions had ever extended to a visit at the Great Farm. I expected that he and Ruth would lead the way, and leave the young lady in my charge, but as Miss Herbert attached herself to my sister, Mr. Marten and I had no alternative but to follow.

Our destination was a large old cottage at the quieter end of the row, which Up-

per Mallowe honoured as its "High Street."
There was a narrow strip of garden in
front, cut in twain by a flagged path leading to the door. At each side of this
door was a wide, latticed window, and there
were three casements on the upper story.
The rector had armed himself with the key
—a very primitive instrument—and in a
moment we were all rambling over the
place, opening doors, and discovering cupboards and shelves, and such-like appliances
of domestic comfort.

"I think it will do," said Ruth.

"You must not say so yet, Miss Garrett,"
returned Mr. Marten; "for you have not
seen its chief beauty." And he ushered us
into a long low room at the back, evidently
an addition to the original building; for it
had no chambers above it. "There!" said
he, "I think that will make such a capital
—what shall we call it, ma'am?—feeding-
room—*salle-à-manger?*"

"So it will," responded Ruth : " the other two rooms can be male and female dormitories, and the floor above wiil do nicely for the housekeeper's home."

" But there are three upper rooms," said Mr. Marten, mounting the stairs, and rapidly opening their doors. " See! two will suffice for the housekeepers, and we shall have one superfluous."

"A great comfort for an ailing woman, or a sick child," I said.

"Certainly," answered Ruth; "and now, Mr. Marten, can you tell us the rent?"

" The landlord has always asked sixteen pounds a year," replied he; "but the cottage has this disadvantage : it is too large and expensive for the poorer class of tenants, and two rough for any others, and so he says he will part with it entirely for one hundred and twenty pounds. What do you think of that offer, Mr. Garrett?"

" I will accept it," I answered; "and then

the remaining expenses will be a small salary for the housekeepers, who will have their rooms rent free, and who need not be wholly without other work, and a little fund for meals, and general assistance for the poor wanderers."

"And furniture?" suggested Miss Herbert, timidly.

"Oh, every bit of that must be begged," said my sister.

The Reverend Lewis Marten put on a very wry face.

"Come, come," said I, "you have made a good beginning already, and you know I am pledged to help you."

"You two look after the money," advised Ruth.

"Do you suppose the village mothers will promise *you* old pans, and kettles, and pillows? Leave those things to us."

"I have read of a very good plan," said that sweet voice, which only spoke too

seldom. " When some good German wished
to furnish an orphan house, he made a
little blank book, and wrote on each leaf
such headings as 'bedding,' 'earthen-
ware,' and so on. Then he sent the
book about, and every one wrote in it
what they would give, and thus each might
be quite sure they were not giving what
was already had."

"Thank you very much, Miss Herbert,"
returned my sister: "that is a good idea.
Whenever anything like that strikes you,
mind you tell us."

"Of course I shall," said Miss Herbert.

" No 'of course' about it," replied Ruth;
" you hesitated before you said that. And
you'll have other wise thoughts come;
but you'll be so afraid they're foolish,
that you'll let us old folks go blundering on without their help. Now, promise
me you wont?"

" I'll try," said the dear girl.

And Ruth looked at her, and gave her head a queer little shake which I could not understand.

"Well, I think we are getting on very well," remarked the clergyman. "I'll just get my memorandum-book, and take a note of our position. But, dear me, I have not a pencil!"

"Oh, I have one," answered Miss Herbert, producing a dainty "lady's companion." Its fastening was a little intricate, and she drew off her gloves to undo it. In the course of this action, I saw something I had not noticed before. On the "engaged" finger she wore a broad, richly-chased gold ring—one of the kind known as "guards."

"Thank you," said Mr. Marten, accepting the proffered pencil. "Now, 'Edward Garrett, Esq., £120'—that looks handsome! Then, 'Miss Ruth Garrett'—what did I understand?" and he glanced archly at my sister.

"You did not understand anything," Ruth retorted. "I've got very little, and I mean to keep it to fill up odd corners where Edward's grand subscription wont go."

"Well, I've written your name," returned Mr. Marten, "and I shall let it stay. Then there's the two old ladies to whom I named the Refuge—Mrs. Withers, one pound one; and Miss Tabitha Vix, five shillings—that's all for the present. Total, one hundred and twenty-one pounds six shillings, and an unknown blank, you see, Miss Garrett."

"Uncle says he will give five pounds," whispered Agnes Herbert.

"Oh, come! this is famous!" said the rector, resuming his notes; "and may I put down anything from you?"

"Half-a-crown, if it's worth while," she said, softly; "and one shilling from Sarah—

that's our servant, Sarah Irons, you know. Perhaps we may get something better out of the lumber-room. Uncle lets us give away anything we find there; but I haven't looked over it for a long time."

"The first thing we have to do," said Ruth, as we left the house, "is to get a good housekeeper, and then we can say, 'Gifts thankfully received at the Refuge.'"

"And who is to hire this housekeeper?" asked Mr. Marten.

"I will, please," responded Ruth. "If you like you may set that down as my subscription. It may prove worth more than Edward's."

Both the clergyman and Miss Herbert resisted our pressing invitation to lunch. So we returned home alone, and Alice admitted us—red-eyed, but smiling, after the parting from her brother.

In the course of the day Ruth paid another visit to the Refuge. She and Alice went

there in the twilight, and stayed some time.
I half guessed the mischief they were plot-
ting, and I was not mistaken. Alice and
her grandfather were appointed hostess and
host at the Refuge.

"It will be so nice to tell in my first
letter to Ewen!" said Alice.

Now you may be sure the opening of this
Refuge made quite a commotion in our
sleepy village of Upper Mallowe—more sen-
sation even than the sudden curtailment of
chanting in St. Cross. The two events
happened simultaneously. Before gossip
could circulate any particulars about the
new "charity," it was announced that the
Reverend Lewis Marten was to preach a
sermon thereon. Out of curiosity, some of
the people who usually walked to the Ritualistic church at Hopleigh, turned their steps
to St. Cross. Also, out of curiosity, some
of the old farmers laid down the local paper,
and went to hear the local discourse. They

found the creaking doors set wide open to receive them, and the bereaved pew-opener's temper was all the sweeter for being spared the trial of the singing-boys in the vestry. The lads themselves, conspicuous by their absence in an official capacity, occupied seats about the church, either under the surveillance of their parents, or steadied by the charge of junior relatives.

The service began. Neither Mr. Marten nor I had exchanged a word on the subject beyond what I have related. He read the sentences and exhortation in his usual clear, ringing tone, and there followed a brief expectant silence. Then he lifted up his voice without the intonation with which he was wont to accompany the chanting. The scattered choir boys, previously instructed, were the first to join, but by the third or fourth petition of our glorious old confession the whole congregation responded. The farmers looked approvingly at each other, and I think the Ritualistic strangers were too surprised to be displeased. The same reform went on throughout the service, and the old people, too blind to read, had the full benefit of those beautiful reassuring psalms, which so marvellously suit every circumstance and experience.

It was the Twenty-second Sunday after Trinity, and the rector took his text from the Gospel for the day. "Shouldest not thou have had compassion on thy fellow-servant, even as I had pity on thee?" His heart was warm with the subject: and his words were eloquent in proportion. As usual, he dwelt strongly on the spiritual wickedness of the world, but only to show the depth of misery from which Christ had saved it. And his closing remarks struck me so much, that I can recall them almost word for word :—

"Christ has forgiven us the ten thousand talents, that dreadful debt which Adam contracted, and which descends to us with accumulating interest. The greatest saint and the greatest sinner are both included in the bond which His mercy remits.

"Yet people rarely realise this brotherhood in evil and misery, this participation in proffered forgiveness. God draws no distinction between sin and crime. The world does. It must. But do not let us say this is because crime injures society, while sin may be left to God, as a matter wholly between Him and the sinner. Crime grows from sin, as the tree springs from its root. Law only punishes crime, simply because sin is too subtle for it. Why, brethren, the sins that really injure society, and from which issue the crimes which fill our prisons and reformatories, are sins to which none of us could truly plead 'Not guilty.' First and foremost is the little seed of self sprouting into wilfulness, and sloth, and apathy. Who has never preferred his own weal to another's, never driven his own will over another's comfort, never held back his hand when he should have stretched it out, or kept silence when he ought to have spoken? If these questions were pressed upon us, who would not be convicted by his own conscience?

"Justice can punish the murderer or the thief, but human justice cannot reach the influences which may have raised his hand against his fellows. Do not suppose these influences excuse his crime. No one need be a victim to circumstances. Circumstance is only given us to conquer. But neither does circumstance excuse the man from whom proceeded the evil influence. Ah, my brethren, when the shadow of a great crime darkens the length and breadth of the land, who of us can safely say, 'I have had no share in this?' A mere want of punctuality or promptitude, by souring tempers, and embittering hearts, may be the first step on the dark road which ends with a gallows! The devil takes care that sin shall be a maze, wherein nobody knows where each path may lead.

"But you will answer, 'Christ came to deliver us from sin.' Truly He came to redeem us from its bondage. He came to show us what we were in Eden, and what we may be again in Paradise. He came to throw the mantle of His own spotless righteousness over the ragged holiness which clothes the purest earthly saint. He came to hold up before us that perfect humanity which fell in fragments round the tree of the knowledge of good and evil. Yes, my brethren, He came to do all this, and what is the result? Those, whom He draws closest to Himself—those, whose purblind souls are so anointed with the balm of His forgiveness, that henceforth they can see clearly—those are the very ones who cry with St. Paul, 'The good that I would, I

do not : but the evil which I would not, that
I do.' Such walk in humility and gentle-
ness, ever watchful lest some unwary stumble
of theirs crush a soul 'for whom Christ
died,' ever praying, 'Lord, pardon us for
the sins which we mistake for virtues !'

"Yes, Christ Himself tells us that 'it
must needs be that offences come.' The
world is God's work, but Satan's tangle is in
it. Every one of us—you and I—have
done our little share to perpetuate that
tangle. And so long as we carry about our
mortality, the devil will sometimes catch
our fingers, and set them at the old mis-
chievous work. But in the meantime we
must put our hands to labour on God's
side. There is always a task ready for
us. Wherever we see pain, or sorrow, or
poverty, or death, let us remember we confront suffering born of sin, *our* sin.

"My brethren, I am about to suggest a
solemn thought. It has been said of some

holy men, that they never knew how much good they did. It may be truly said of all of us, that we know not what evil we have caused. You, the regular worshipper and communicant, some permanent inconsistency in your life may have given a forgotten acquaintance a lasting prejudice against religion. You, parents, bewailing rebellious children, perhaps you 'provoked' them to wrath and sin. You, neglected wives, by your own peevishness and self-consideration may have alienated the love which you should have held next to God's. I, myself, lamenting over the empty seats I too often see in this temple, may have driven my flock away by my own coldness and apathy! And alas! alas! my brethren, the evil our own hands have done, our own hands cannot always undo. Those whom we injure, die or go beyond our influence. There are words and deeds which we cannot recollect without remorse, yet which can never be

cancelled. Then, as we pray that other
hands may efface our wrong-doing, let us remember that some may be so praying on
behalf of one whom we can succour, either
in mind or body. How happy we should
be to hear that God had permitted a good
man to destroy our evil work! So, let us
be up and doing, that in our turn, with
God's blessing, we may confer that happiness on others. Let it no more be said that
the homeless, the erring, or the miserable,
pass among us unsheltered, uncounselled,
and uncheered. Christmas again draws
near—to some of us it will be brighter than
ever before ; to others its earthly brightness
may be departed. But the gayest, as well
as the poorest, and the saddest, and the
utterly bereaved, will be none the worse for
winning 'the blessing of those that were
ready to perish.'"

Mr. Marten spoke so earnestly and
pointedly, that the interest of the most

sluggish was aroused, and the church was
solemn with the breathless silence of rapt
attention.   There was but one interruption.
When the rector's warning touched on
family miseries, Mr. Herbert suddenly rose,
left his seat, and walked down the aisle.
At the font, however, he paused, passed his
hand reflectively over his whiskers, and
returned to his pew.   But immediately after
the final benediction, and before any one
had risen from prayer, he and his niece both
left the building.

There was a collection made at the door,
and when we passed out, the "plates"
seemed in a tolerably prosperous condition.
The rough church-path was not so clear as
on my first visit to St. Cross, for neighbours were lingering to greet other neighbours whom they had not seen there
for a long time.   As we went through
the crowd I heard many remarks such as
these :—

"Parson gave us a moighty fine sermon. He seems quite awaukened up."

"Ay, you may say that! He spoke as if he meant it."

"A'most as if he wor preachin' to some 'un there, and knew ezactly what they wanted."

"Perhaps he wor."

Next day when Mr. Marten came to confess his mistake, and to own that the people of Upper Mallowe had proved liberal beyond his hopes, I told him this. He smiled at the rough criticism, but his reply was—

"They were right. I was preaching at some one,—at myself. All the time I bore in mind my miserable blunder with that poor fellow, Ewen."

"Ah, you had a visit from him before he left for London," said Ruth.

"So I had," he answered.

"And what did you say?" inquired my sister.

"We each begged the other's pardon," returned the rector, "and I think he'll count me among the friends he has left at Upper Mallowe,—or at least not among the enemies. He is not at all an ordinary chip of humanity. You did a great work in saving him, Mr. Garrett."

"Edward just did a common Christian duty," said Ruth; "if God bless it, to Him be all the glory!"

"And you think the people felt my sermon last Sunday?" queried Mr. Marten, presently.

"Yes, just because your heart was in every word," I answered.

"I feared I was, as usual, too gloomy and severe," he remarked.

"No, no," said I; "you own you were preaching at yourself,—therefore you loved the sinner, understood his errors, and felt a human pity for his remorse. Now, you must ask God to enlarge your sympathies till you can do the same in every case, and then your severity will be only truthful love."

" And if your preaching suits your own heart, it will certainly suit somebody else," added Ruth.

CHAPTER VII.

GEORGE WILMOT FROM LONDON.

AND thus Christmas drew near. By that time the Refuge was fairly established, Miss Herbert's "Contribution Book" having secured sundry very useful gifts, which went far to spare our little cash account, and Mr. M'Callum and Alice were settled in their new abode—both made exceedingly happy by punctual and comfortable letters from Ewen. And so Ruth and I jogged on in our quiet way.

But we saw very little of Agnes. She helped my sister in all the Refuge arrangements, yet we could not allure her to our house for a leisurely visit, nor even detain her for such when she made a call. She was always quite anxious to return home, as if it were some post of imperative duty, from which absence was absolutely desertion.

"How shall we keep Christmas, Ruth?" I asked, one evening in December.

"Just like a Thanksgiving Sunday, I suppose," said she. "There are no children coming home for the holidays."

Now, of course I knew that. But Ruth will say things.

"Christmas is a birthday feast," I remarked, "and so it should be kept."

"Ah, but birthdays are drear times," she answered, "when there's no one to stoop over us and give us a kiss and a keepsake."

"I suppose that is why old people leave off keeping them," I said. "I think they are wrong; let them rather give kisses and keepsakes on the dear date when they used to receive them. So with Christmas. Ah,

Ruth, you were mistaken when you said we had no child to gladden us at this season. Is there not a Babe in a manger at Bethlehem which is ours for ever?"

Ruth did not reply. She never replies to such remarks. I believe she thinks the more for her silence, for by-and-by she said—

"Then what should you like to do on Christmas Day?"

"I want to give as many little bits of pleasure as I can," I replied; "such little bits of pleasure as made me happy when I was a boy, Ruth."

"Ah, you were easy to please, Edward," said she; "and a very good thing, too!"

"Any one who can be pleased at all is as pleased with little as with much," I replied. "A Christmas card gives as much delight as a Christmas-box. A child is as charmed with the discovery of a blackberry bush, as is a miner with his nugget. And perhaps the one 'find' is as valuable as the other."

"To the child, may be; but not to the man," retorted Ruth. "Recollect, grown-up people have no leisure to go blackberry-hunting unless they've first got a nugget of their own, or are degraded enough to live on other people. Don't you pretend to undervalue money, Edward. It's God's gift as much as anything else. It depends on us whether it be a blessing or a curse."

"That is how you always pull me up when I grow poetical," I said, smiling.

"Talking rubbish is not poetical," she answered. "Sham sentiment is too often mistaken for poetry, and when people find common-life tears off such rags as she goes along, they foolishly fancy they are too fine for every-day wear, and so put aside the tinsel for best occasions. Now real poetry is just naked truth."

"You are far too clever to argue with, Ruth," said I.

"Ah, you see I kept a circulating library, and the best books were always at home," she remarked, drily.

Presently, being really willing to fall in with my humble plans, she observed—

"But a little consideration makes money go very far in giving pleasure. It prevents you sending coals to a widow at Newcastle, or presenting a farmer with a turkey, or a schoolboy with Euclid, or a blind man with a tract."

"That is to the point, Ruth," I said; "now I just want to give a little bit of genuine delight to every one I know. I wish you had second sight, and could reveal the secret desire of each friend and neighbour."

"Then you would find out you could satisfy none," she returned. "Do you think folks are so shallow as to long for aught you could send as a Christmas gift?"

"No," I answered; "but everyone has some dear little wish, whose gratification makes the great want easier to bear."

"You are right there," responded my sister. "If you cannot give a man dinner, you may give him a biscuit for lunch."

"We must send some pretty surprise to every house which has young folks," I said.

"And we must not let them find out where it comes from," added Ruth. "Nobody will set greater value on anything because sent by you or me, Edward. If they cannot guess the giver, it will make them feel kindly towards all their friends."

"But yet we cannot tell what will please each child," I remarked.

"A book or a picture with a little innocent mystery about it will satisfy all the young people," answered Ruth. "It will

be harder to hit the fancy of the elder
ones."

"The elder ones will be pleased in the
young one's pleasure," I said; "and as I
find there will be cheap railway excursions
to and from London at Christmas-time, I
shall buy a return-ticket and send it to
Ewen, and his arrival on Christmas morning
shall be my gift to that family."

"Bravo, Edward," exclaimed my sister,
"that is just the right thing. You are
cleverer than I am, in your own way."

"Only you think it a small sort of way,"
I said, laughing.

"As you know my thoughts, I'll not con-
tradict you," said she. "And what shall
we do for Mr. Marten?"

"Ask him to dinner?" I queried.

Ruth shook her head. "Very likely
he would have somewhere better to go,"
she said, "though he might come, thinking
to please us; while, for my own part, I'd

rather have only ghosts at the Christmas-table."

And yet you have never known the bitter changes which some know," I remarked. "You can only miss our father and our mother, and they were spared till their time was fully ripe."

"I know the changes in myself," Ruth answered. "It's my own ghost that comes to see me on feast-days."

"But you would not object to any guest who had nowhere else to go?" I asked.

"Certainly not," she said; "such a presence would lay the ghost. Not that I wish it laid. I like to see what a fool I was once. I only wish I could be such a fool now!"

"Age is higher and happier than youth," I remarked, harping on my pet theory.

"I know it," she answered; "but yet some folks like climbing mountains better than sitting at rest. You must not judge every one by yourself, Edward."

"I wish I could guess what would please Agnes Herbert," I said, presently.

"If we only knew what ailed the girl!" observed Ruth.

We little dreamed who was then walking across our garden. We heard the back door slammed, and in a moment Phillis appeared in the parlour, announcing that a gentleman had brought a little ragged boy to our gate, and had bidden him ask for Mr. Garrett.

"Is the gentleman in the kitchen? Who is he?" asked Ruth, rising, in astonishment.

"Please, ma'am, I could not see him out in the dark," answered the sapient Phillis, "and he wouldn't wait; but says he to the boy, when I opened the gate, 'You're all right now,' says he. And, please, sir, the boy seems stupefied-like."

"It's only some stranger who has heard

of us in connexion with the Refuge," said
I. " Is the lad in the kitchen, Phillis ?"

" I've kept him out in the passage,"
replied Phillis; "for it's a bad night, and
he's awful muddy, and would muck the
kitchen-floor, if you please, sir."

" No, I'm not pleased, Phillis," I answered.
" If cleanliness is to follow godliness, then
kindliness must keep between."

" Ask the boy to the fire directly," said
practical Ruth, " at the same time let him
rub his feet well upon the mat."

" This is a queer adventure," I commented, as the girl obediently departed,
and we prepared to follow.

" I daresay it will put your Christmas
cards and keepsakes right out of your head,"
said Ruth.

" A very good suggestion," I retorted.
" Your doubt will help me to remember
them, my sister."

We found the boy seated by the kitchen-hearth, with his dirty feet tucked up on the rung of the Windsor chair, perhaps by Phillis' directions. He seemed a coarse, vulgar, neglected lad, and he gave an introductory snivel when he saw us. Of course he was a scrap of God's writing, but the divine characters were sadly blurred.

"Do you want to speak with me—Mr. Garrett?" I asked, taking a seat opposite him.

"The gen'leman said so," he answered.

"What have you to say?" I inquired.

"I dunno," he replied, hopelessly, whirling his thick, dirty hands; "only the gen'leman said, 'Then, you're all right now.'"

We had heard as much from Phillis.

"Who was the gentleman?" I questioned.

"I dunno," replied the boy.

"What were you doing when he spoke to you?" asked Ruth. Her clear, quick tones penetrated his thick skull deeper than mine. I fancy they had a magisterial echo, for he instantly thrust his red fore-finger into his bleared eye, and jerked out whiningly, " I warn't a-doing of no harm. I only arst him for a penny."

" You're a stranger here," remarked Ruth, in the same sharp voice, which seemed to keep his mind awake ; " where do you come from ?"

" I comed from Lunnon—I tramped it," he answered ; " mother only died this day was a week."

He did not look so vulgar and coarse when one heard that history. God help the boy !

" What brought you here ?" asked Ruth.

" Mother said father was summat here : he'd run away from her, years ago. She niver wanted to be arter him herself, but she bid me look to him, when she wor gone."

" What is his name ?" I inquired.

"George Wilmot," said the lad, "and that's mine too."

"I don't believe there's such a name in the place, sir," said Phillis, aside.

"You say you asked the gentleman for a penny," pursued Ruth; "then what did he answer?"

"Please, he catched me by the shoulder, an' turned me round, an' stared at me for a minute or two, and didn't say nothin'."

"Not at first, perhaps," continued Ruth, "but what did he say when he spoke?"

"He said 'God help us!' just like mother used; and then he asked my name," said the boy.

"And then?" queried Ruth.

"Then he said, 'I haven't anything to give you.' But he kep' hold o' my shoulder, an' I walked along with him, till he says, 'Where are you going to-night?' And I tolled him I must sleep under an 'edge or

summat. And he says, 'God help us!'
again; and fell a-thinking like."

" What made him bring you here ?" asked
my sister.

" Well, he says, ' By-the-bye, there's a
Refuge somewhere near,' and asked if I
knew what a Refuge meant, and I said,
'Didn't I!' An' then he stood still and
looked about, and says, 'I've never seen it,
and don't know where it is, but I'll take
you to the good people who opened it;' and
then he went on muttering about devils
giving kind folk a deal to undo, which I
couldn't make out. He told me this was
the house as we came to the gate, but says
he, ' We'll go round the other way, for I'm
fittest for back doors now,' and he laughed
out, ' Ha! ha! ha!' "

The bright fire was evidently thawing the
lad's frozen wits, for he gave his last words
in another tone, in imitation of his strange
guide.

"Should your know you father if you saw him?" inquired Ruth.

The boy shook his head: "He's not been nigh us sin' I wor a babby," he said.

"What was this gentleman like?" queried my suspicious sister.

"Tall," answered the boy, "and he had on a cloak."

"Was he young or old?" asked Ruth.

"I dunno, ma'am," staring as if the answer was quite beyond his powers. It was the first time he gave my sister a respectful title. I believe he thought her question showed a high opinion of his faculties, and so honoured her accordingly.

"Was he as old as your mother, do you think?" pursued Ruth, after a moment's reflection.

"Oh, no," said the boy, grinning at the idea, "*she* was quite an old woman—she allays said so!"

"What was her age?" inquired Ruth,

trying to get at the truth by a side-path.

"Thirty-three," replied the lad succinctly.

Ruth glanced at me with elevated eye-brows; this was her first experience of the statistics of a London street-boy.

"When did you have anything to eat?" I asked.

"A baker gaved me a clump o' bread this morning, it was not a right dinner, to say," he answered; "but coming along past the public, the hostler had a half-empty pot, and he telled me I might drink it up. That was good," he added, smacking his lips at the recollection.

O Thou Father of kings and beggars, which thanksgiving makes the sweetest incense before Thy throne,—the formal calling upon Thy name of one who is discontented with his venison, or the gladness of another who picketh up the coarsest crumbs of Dives' table, and thanketh

Thee ignorantly, as do the beasts and birds ?"

Phillis instantly brought forth a loaf and some cold meat. I am thankful to say, she understood her master sufficiently to do this without asking direct permission.

I resolved to take the lad to the Refuge myself. The M'Callums were old inhabitants, of intelligence far superior to Phillis, and they might know some clue whereby to discover the boy's runagate father. I had a faint idea of my own in this matter, a most unreasonable one, inasmuch as it was attached, not to the cognomen "Wilmot," but to the simple name "George," which my common sense told me might belong to a dozen men in Upper Mallowe.

The lad made a considerable supper, without taking long in the process, and then we started off together. Ruth's questions had given him the notion that we took some interest in the stranger who had brought him to us. So as we trudged along he suggested, "Mayhap the gentleman will be about yet."

"Whereabouts did you meet him?" I asked.

"Just here," he answered.

Now at that instant we passed the Great Farm.

We were not long in reaching the Refuge, and Alice promptly admitted us, and led us to her little sitting room on the upper floor. From Ruth's accounts, I knew that she used this chamber as her sleeping apartment, the other being occupied by her grandfather, while the third, by Alice's own wish, was kept for such extra uses as might arise from the necessities of the Refuge.

"Grandfather is down-stairs," she explained: "there are two poor men here for the night, and he's in the upper room, talking with them. Shall I fetch him, sir?"

"If you please, Alice," I said; "but you may promise that I shall not keep him long."

The old man soon presented himself, with that cheery face, which must have beamed on the poor refugees like a sudden sunrise after a dreary night. I hastened to inquire if he knew any one in the village called George Wilmot.

Mr. M'Callum shook his head.

Alice said, " No."

"Do you remember such a name at any time ?" I inquired.

Neither of them could. So I called the boy forward, and made him repeat his story.

"Hech, sirs! but it's a waefu' tale," said the good old Scotchman. "I'm thinking the laddie had best bide here the nicht, and look aboot you the morn. He'll maybe hae to bide here a wee, sae ye'd best mak' his bed i' the little room, Alie.

And if he gaes doon stairs, he'll find some warm parritch; and the twa puir callants below are nae sic bad company."

"He's had some supper already," I observed, as the boy seemed disposed to obey with extraordinary alacrity.

"Ou, ay, sir," replied Mr. M'Callum; "but a little het parritch canna do him ony harm. Let the laddie gae. Ye see, sir," he continued, when we heard the supper-room door close behind the boy, " I wadna hint a dispareeging thing afore the bairn's face. Let him think o' his father as weel's he can; but, verralike, if he were George Wilmot when he married, he wasna George Wilmot after he ran awa'. The man that does ae base thing is fit for anither."

"But was it not strange about the gentleman in the lane?" observed Alice, who was engaged at the cupboard, searching for blankets.

"At first, I wondered whether he were the father," I said. "His strange kind-ness might be the working of remorse."

Mr. M'Callum shook his head.

"Differin' natures hae differin' remorses," he remarked. "A cauld-bluided scoondrel, wha didna ken gif his bairn had starved or no, would be verra unlikely to fash where the lad passed ae nicht. Maist like, sic a one would say to himself—'Gif the laddie's used to it, the way-side's as guid to him as my bedroom to me.' That's the way the deevil com-forts his ain while they're his. He doesna trouble them much, till God gets a grip o' them. An' if God had got a grip o' him—bein', as he waur, the father—I dinna think he'd hae left his lang-lost bairn to strangers, e'en to their tender mercies. Maist like, the gentleman is just some puir misguided callant, wha has gotten the wrang bit in his mouth—

else why fittest for back-doors, sir?—-but hasna travelled the deevil's road lang eneuch to like to see ithers gangin' the same gait. Sic a one feels anguishes of remorse—and that's just God's grip, sir."

"But Judas himself felt remorse," I observed, getting into the argument.

"And went and hangit himsel'," said he; "and sae do mony mair. Gif they would but bide a wee! Why, sir, ye'll nae say Christ's death hadna poo'r to save the puir traitor? Only the misguided creature went and hangit himsel'."

And so we sat and conversed till George Wilmot came up from his "parritch," and Alice returned from making his bed.

"Now, my boy," I began, "what did your mother say about your father—what did she bid you say when you should see him?"

"She said she was afeared he'd taken her

in mighty; but there was no telling," replied the lad; "and if I got to see him, I was to give him this." And he produced a folded paper, dirty and worn, which he handed to me. "Mother took a long whiles a-writin' it," he remarked, "and she used to say perhaps father a-tired of her, because he was a famous scholard. I can't read what she writ; but may be you will, sir," he added.

I took the letter reverently; for it seemed like a secret between the dead and the living. I paused before I unfolded it; but the boy repeated his request, and, indeed, to peruse it seemed the best way towards fulfilling the deserted woman's wish. This was the contents. I will not translate the strange spelling and bad grammar. They have a pathos with which I dare not meddle.

"MY DERE GEORGE,

"Why did you leve me without a wurd, this is writ to saye that i furgive yu, and hope whe shall meet in Heven, i was not good enuf for yu, but yu dident say so, when yu cam cortin me ovar master's gate, and all the gals grudgin my fortin for yu was a fine gentelman. When yu git this, I am ded and shall not trobble yu never no more. but yu aught luke to your pore boy, wich as bin a good boy to his mother, and fur his sake, i'm niver sorry I maared yu, so don't yu think it. This comes, hopeing yu are well from your luving wife

"MARY WILMOT."

I took a little time to decipher this letter; indeed, my sight failed over it. But when I had done, the boy said simply, "Wont ye read it out, sir? She read it to me, she did, and it'll be like hearin' her speak oncet more."

So I read it.   And the great rough boy sobbed out loud.   God's writing was clear enough upon his heart.   I shook hands with him when I came away, but I did not say one word to "deepen the effect" of that letter.   As soon would I have interrupted the dead mother had she stood among us in the spirit and spoken to her boy.

Alice conducted me to the door.   The moon was shining brightly, and cast its blueness over her face.   As she stood on the threshold, she said in a whisper—"Isn't it strange that none of us can recollect a Wilmot in these parts?"

"Not so strange, if your grandfather guesses rightly," I answered.

"*His* name—you know whose, sir?—was George," she murmured.

I started at this suggestion of my own thought; but reflected in another's mind, I could see its absurdity.   So I said, merrily—

" And so is Mr. Smith's the chemist, and
Mr. Tozer's the baker. No, no, Alice, it's a
bad habit to make out coincidences. It
does no good, for we can't trust them,
unless they're based on facts, and if we've
got the facts, then we don't want the coincidences. But, by the way, your remark
reminds me that I never heard the surname
of that unhappy man?"

" It was Roper—George Roper, sir," she
answered.

" Thank you—for, considering the interest I feel in Ewen, it was awkward not
to know it. But what are these sounds?"—
for from the back of the house came a voice
singing a spirited song, accompanied by
divers notes as from some uncertain and
feeble instrument.

Alice laughed—a pleasant, soft laugh—
" It's only the two ' refugees' (so we call our
pensioners), one is singing and the other is
piping with a bit of paper on a comb. They

often do it, when they're not over tired with tramping, sir."

I wonder if any rigid philanthropist would think such doings a breach of "the order and discipline of a charitable institution." I only stood and listened. I have no ear for music, but as I caught the stirring words—

> " Hearts of oak are our ships,
>   Jolly tars are our men ;
>   We always are ready,
>   Steady, boys ! steady !
> We'll fight and we'll conquer again and again"—

I was quite satisfied with the performance. Why should we think our kindness best repaid by long faces and dead silence? Is it not unreasonable to forbid a song because we have given a supper? I remembered a great "human naturalist" said it was a happy omen for the country when the beggar was as content with his dish as the lord with his land. Better to keep our charity than to sell it at the price of enjoyment.

"There! that's grandfather gone to them," said Alice.

"He wont stop the song?" I queried.

"Oh, no, sir," she answered; "most likely he'll join in the chorus. He's fond of singing a song himself. But he thinks it's right to go in and out of the room in a friendly way. And when he's told them stories and anecdotes, and talked pleasantly, there's few so hard as to take it unkindly when he gets out the Bible, before going to bed."

I went home with a heart full of pleasant feelings. I had not forgotten my " cards and keepsakes," as Ruth warned me I should. So every time I passed a village boy, I thought, " Ah, my fine fellow, there's a 'tip' coming for you!" and then the Upper Mallowe boys appeared in my eyes uncommonly nice boys. And it was solemnly sweet to think of true-hearted Mary Wilmot in her London pauper grave —no, not there, but in heaven ; for are not our trespasses forgiven, as we forgive those who trespass against us? And it was odd that her boy should come among us like a guest at Christmas time. Have not some " entertained angels unawares?" and in that case, they cannot look as we fancy angels, or they would carry their welcome with them. I don't suppose the lad is any less like an angel, because he knows the price of boy-labour in the docks, and how little one can live upon down Stepney way, and what it is to be hungry and tired—nay, there is One, higher than the angels, who knows all about that, and was a good son to his parents in a carpenter's shop at Nazareth.

But as I entered our house a hearty voice recalled me to the world of snug suppers and warm beds, for Ruth exclaimed, "Here you are at last, Edward. Come to your supper, and don't run all over the world, fancying you are as young as ever!"

CHAPTER VIII.

A CHRISTMAS CONFIDENCE.

GEORGE WILMOT was still in the Refuge when Christmas Day came. There was quite a bustle in our house on the Eve. With Mr Marten's help I got off my presents, a most miscellaneous heap—tea, tobacco, knick-knacks, pictures, cards, and books; the last three items all so pretty that if I had not wished to give them I should have liked to keep them! The Rector was in high spirits, having an invitation to dine next day at a mansion a few miles off, inhabited by an old naval officer and his only daughter,—a fact from which I drew my own inferences. As Ruth could not let this hospitable season pass without a little delicate meddling in culinary matters, a spicy perfume pervaded the parlour, and contributed to the general feeling of festivity and good-will.

Perhaps that was the gayest bit of our Christmas keeping. The day was a quiet one in our house. Even Phillis was away, for Ruth gave her permission to rejoin her own family; and only our new servant, who was a stranger in the village, remained to wait upon us. We did not venture to invite any guests. It is cruel to allure family-people from their homes at such a season; and so far as we could ascertain, all the single folk of Upper Mallowe were already happily appropriated.

But as we took our places at the breakfast-table, a sound of sweet singing startled the clear morning air. Looking from the window, we saw the choir-boys of St. Cross standing round our garden-gate. It was no unfamiliar chorale which they sang, but just the dear Christmas hymn, "Hark, the herald angels sing." There are some old tunes which have such an echo in the universal heart that I sometimes fancy we shall use them in our heavenly praises.

When they ceased I went out and thanked the lads, and wished them a merry Christmas. I singled out the leader, and wanted to give him five shillings to divide among the rest. I hope the moralists will not say I was making them mercenary. Whenever I receive a pleasure I long to do something in return. But the boy said, quite sedately, that Mr. Marten told them to do it, because I was doing so much to the village. Now here was a poser! I must accept their gratuitous service because it was grateful. Yet I could not put away the five shillings. A bright thought came.

"Come, my boys," I said, " I thank you very heartily for your remembrance of an

old man; and as you have given me such
pleasure, I should like others to have as
much. Go to the Great Farm, and sing
your hymn again, and take these five
shillings in consideration of so employing
your valuable time." And as I did not
wish to argue through any further remon-
strance from that sedate elder boy, I ran
back to the house, and the young choristers
set up a cheer.

Ruth and I went to church, and found it
quite gay with holly and laurel; and the
whole service, to the very tones of the
rector's voice, was of a jubilant character.
So Christmas services should be: especially
for the sake of those who may have little
rejoicing elsewhere. The sermon was very
short and very bright, being from that
seasonable text in the eighth chapter of
Nehemiah, "Go your way, eat the fat, and
drink the sweet, and send portions unto
them for whom nothing is prepared: for

this day is holy unto our Lord; neither be ye sorry, for the joy of the Lord is your strength."

Somehow (I say this in parenthesis), I fancied that Mr. Marten's Christmas visit was an unexpected happiness to the young man. But he had been less desponding in his views for some time. And God occasionally rewards our efforts by sending a blessing which makes them easier.

Mr. Herbert and his niece were in their pew. Agnes looked as if she had been crying. I think the very gladness of the hymns and sermon tried her. The old people liked it: the acute agonies had died out of their lives, and then joy is as sunshine on an old, well-remembered grave, which one hopes soon to share. But to sorrowful youth it comes like spring sunlight on the face of yesterday's dead. God help the young!

They hurried out of church before us,

though they paused to exchange seasonable wishes over the pew-door. But all the M'Callums waited for us in the graveyard— the grandfather and Alice perfectly radiant with delight at Ewen's unexpected arrival. The young man himself seemed much more happy and open-hearted for his residence among people who did not suspect and shun him, and was quite eager to deliver the many kind messages he brought me from the good folks in my old house of business. Now, I knew these worthy people would not have sent these messages by him if they had not liked him. So I augured well for Ewen.

Ruth and I dined very cheerfully together, and afterwards I amused myself by droning over my holiday-books, by which I mean sundry smart volumes of the poets, that I received as school-prizes in those remote ages when I was a boy. Their glories are rather faded now—like mine! Ruth occupied herself with idleness till tea-time—it must have been hard work for her. Afterwards, being incapable of further exertion in that way, I found her seated opposite me, with linen sleeves drawn over her silk ones, and a grand red and blue china bowl before her, busily cutting up candied peels for the New-Year's cake.

"Is not that the maid's duty?" I asked, heedlessly.

"Household affairs are every woman's study," she replied, cutting energetically.

Now I like to watch an educated woman at domestic work. She makes it beautiful. So I said, "Women are never more pleasing than when so engaged."

"They are never more dignified," returned Ruth.

"Certainly it is their hereditary empire, where they reign undisputed," I remarked.

"If they leave that throne, they may wish for another!" responded my sister.

"Oh, I think in other spheres, they may at least dispute male pre-eminence," I observed.

"Let them, if they like," said Ruth; "the more simpletons in the world, the better for wise people. Let who likes take pride in working out fantastic problems like any common school-boy, there will still remain some sensible women to get dinner and keep house."

"But should women have no mental discipline?" I queried.

"Mental discipline!" she echoed, "the wise woman of the Proverbs got hers through her needlework and housewifery. All the 'ologies' in the world will never make greater women than we have had without them."

"But some women are called out of the shelter of home," I remarked.

"Don't say 'called out,'" answered my sister, quickly, "the very duty they owe to home sometimes *sends* them out. A woman may do out-of-the-way tasks for very womanly reasons (a touch of pathos in her voice— then, with a spark of satire), " and it's only foolish men who can't understand that !"

"Certainly, I am sorry that the phrase 'strong-minded,' in itself a compliment, is now perverted to describe women who bring contempt on their sex," I observed.

" I'm afraid a strong mind wont support a woman very far," returned Ruth; " but if she have a strong heart, I'll trust her wherever duty calls her."

"I really do not think brave women cry out for their rights," I said.

"I should think not," answered my sister, indignantly. " Courage does not exaggerate wrongs: cowardice does. Only weak women wish to be placed in rivalry with men; and when men accordingly treat them as they would other rivals, thy cry, 'Shame! shame!' and wonder what has become of the ancient chivalry."

" Well, I must say I think them greatly mistaken when they aspire to rule rather than to serve," I remarked.

Ruth smiled peculiarly : " Christ set the fashion of ruling by service," she answered ; " ' ICH DIEN,' is a royal motto."

And that set me thinking. Certainly in this present, I defer to my sister, and would do anything to gratify her wishes. I am master of the house and the cash-box, yet I like best to hold my dominion as her viceroy. And why? Because I remember how she has toiled for me; how in the old past she may have sacrificed for my sake far more than I can ever know till all secrets be revealed in heaven. And, oh, when we remember that there all the secrets of holy lives will be made known, we can well understand the perfect love that shall reign among glorified spirits. But that bright picture has also a terrible reverse.

As I looked at Ruth cutting her candied

peel, it struck me that a self-sacrificing life seems an elixir of true youth. I wish more women would try it. I am sure they would find it answer far better than their balms and kalydors.

"I think you would have made an uncommonly good wife, Ruth," I said presently.

"A new discovery, eh, Edward?"—this very drily.

"Well—you know—I used to think that as you were such a clever woman of business, perhaps——"

"So long as men think idiots make the best wives, I hope they'll get them," she retorted. "It's a pity you didn't try the experiment yourself."

And there was silence till Ruth finished her peels, put aside the red and blue bowl, and folded her hands on her lap.

"Well, my sister, we have had a happy Christmas Day," I said, softly.

Yes," she answered, with a nod, "we've done with merry ones."

"We've got their memory still," I suggested.

"And don't we remember them well!" she said, eagerly. "I can forget fifty years in a minute, and fancy that we're again at the little parties in the Clockhouse. Half the year we expected those parties, and the other half we talked them over. Boys and girls don't get so much good out of their pleasures now-a-days."

"How few who shared those festivities remain within our reach!" I sighed. "Did you go to those parties long after I left home, Ruth?"

"Never," she answered.

"Why, how was that?" I asked.

"I had grown an old woman," she said, gazing into the fire.

"What! at eighteen?" I queried.

"Yes, at eighteen," she replied, turning to me with a strange smile.

Would I ask any more questions? No. I would as soon startle a sanctuary by noisy importunities. If my sister chose, I could wait for more perfect knowledge of her till our angels stood side by side in a safer home.

"Do you remember the Carewes?" she inquired presently.

"What, the girl with the golden locks and the boy with a red shock head, who used to play the piano?" I said.

"I suppose you mean the right pair," she answered; "but Richard Carewe's hair was auburn, not red, and his sister's curls were more like tinsel than gold."

"I remember her. Like all the village boys, I thought her very pretty; but, as I recall her beauty now, I think it was meretricious, like half-spoiled false jewellery. She was no favourite of yours, I recollect. What has put her in your head?"

"Simply because I see by her gravestone

at St. Cross that she was our Mr. Herbert's mother," replied Ruth.

" And did you never hear of her marriage," I asked, "when Upper and Lower Mallowe lie so close together?"

"Laura Carewe's friends were not mine," said Ruth. "How such a shallow and selfish girl was her brother's sister, I could never understand."

"And what became of Richard?" I inquired.

"Richard died," said Ruth, quietly; "he died in London on the very day you entered it."

"Dear me!" I said, somehow awed by my sister's tone. "He was a sort of genius, was he not?"

"He was a genius," returned Ruth. "I have no ear for music—no more than you have, Edward, and you know what that means—but he could make me cry the moment he touched the keys."

" I suppose he went to London to try his fortune," I observed.

" Yes," said Ruth; " and of course he was unfortunate at first, like everybody else. And it is not in the purest or pleasantest places that musicians often begin their career. And there was wild blood in those Carewes. And Richard got into trouble, and was put into the debtors' prison. Laura was older than he : they were orphans, and their father had willed that all the little family property should go to purchase an annuity for her. But she never went near her brother in the cell, only made senti- mental suffering for herself out of his misery. And at last, his creditor was kinder than his sister, and Richard got his liberty ; but only to die on a doorstep, Edward—only to die on a doorstep, in the broad light of the sun !"

" But his misfortunes came out of his faults, Ruth," I said, very gently, for I quite understood the solemn monotony of her voice.

"I know they did," she answered; "but if God sent all our faults the misfortunes which they merit, where should we be? And so little might have saved him!"

"There seemed a something familiar in Agnes' face the moment I saw her," added Ruth presently. "I can understand it now. She is Laura Carewe's grand-daughter, but she has Richard Carewe's eyes."

"Did Laura have other children besides our Mr. Herbert and Agnes' father?" I asked.

"I have only heard of those; but she may have had others for aught I know," said Ruth.

And there followed a long, long silence. This, then, was my sister's romance. She would never say so—never do more than tell the common-place story in simple words and solemn tones,—perhaps she had never done so much before. And yet what a new light it shed on all her character! I glanced at her, and it seemed that I must have been blind not to have seen some such history written in her face.

"Was Richard buried in London," I asked, at last.

"Yes," she answered, "and God only knows where! I humbled myself to inquire of Laura, but she could not tell—only she said it was some pauper burial-ground, and she went into hysterics at the idea!"

My proud, patient sister! It was a bitter memory of first love—the fiery, wasted genius in a beggar's grave. How sadly different from mine—that innocent, holy girl, laid with reverent affection in the tomb of her fathers. And so I am happy in the knowledge that those who sleep with Jesus reign with Him in glory, while Ruth takes heart, remembering who said to the dying thief, "This day thou shalt be

with me in paradise." Verily God plants
some comfort in every soil.

"This has been quite a Christmas talk,"
exclaimed Ruth, rousing herself, with a dim
smile.

"My poor dear sister!" I said, laying my
hand upon hers.

She shook it off as if it pained her.
"What's the matter with you?" she asked,
starting from her seat her old, erect self.
"I daresay you want your supper. I'll go
and see after it."

And when she returned, the history had
vanished from her face, and the whole conversation seemed like a dream!

END OF VOL. I.

LONDON :

SAVILL, EDWARDS AND CO., PRINTERS, CHANDOS STREET,

COVENT GARDEN.

CLARISSA:

A NOVEL. BY SAMUEL RICHARDSON.

Edited by E. S. DALLAS, Author of "THE GAY SCIENCE."

In Three Volumes.

Extract from Editor's Preface.

" . . . No one who is familiar with 'Clarissa' can wonder at Macaulay's admiration of it, nor be unprepared for his account of its fascinating influence. He knew it almost by heart. It is the finest work of fiction ever written in any language, said Sir James Mackintosh. He who was our first novelist in point of time, has in fact produced our first novel in point of rank. And not only is this opinion the final outcome of English, it is also the settled faith of French, criticism. The French are our chief rivals in prose fiction; and their opinion of 'Clarissa' is summed up in the saying of Alfred de Musset, that it is—*le premier roman du monde.* They have nearly without exception regarded Richardson as incomparable, and his chief romance as one of the greatest marvels of art. Rousseau declared that nothing equal to 'Clarissa' or approaching it was ever written in any language; and on the death of its author Diderot pronounced his panegyric in terms of the utmost enthusiasm.

" I have ventured to offer to English readers a revised edition of the marvellous tale,—matchless in the range of prose fiction,—because, for the honour of our literature, I lament that the noblest of all novels, the most pathetic and the most sublime, should be unread and well-nigh unknown among us; and because I agree with the French critics in thinking that the prolixity which has been its bane may be diminished with an advantage to which there is no serious drawback."

NEW NOVEL: by the Author of " The Woman in White."

THE MOONSTONE:

BY WILKIE COLLINS.

In Three Volumes.

From The Daily Telegraph.

"This is a wonderful book, surpassingly clever, and absorbingly interesting. It ought to be read, and would certainly be enjoyed alike, by two very different classes—those who scarcely ever read novels, and those who spend nearly their entire life in devouring them. It would be impossible to do bare justice to Mr. Wilkie Collins without going even so far as to declare that, in his own branch of art, he is almost, if not absolutely perfect. . . . . We have by no means exhausted all that we could say in praise of 'The Moonstone;' and it would take us a long time to do so. We will therefore conclude by saying that anybody who omits to read it voluntarily denies himself one of the greatest mental treats in which it is possible for a man or woman to indulge."

TINSLEY BROTHERS, 18, CATHERINE STREET, STRAND.